D

Whirling, Amos Spack backhanded Maxine across the face. Maxine was jarred backward. Toad and Charlie Grub turned to watch, and that was when Fargo struck.

Wrenching free of Toad's hold on his wrist, he grabbed a stake and thrust the tapered end into Toad's neck. The stake wasn't all that sharp, but it was sharp enough to pierce soft flesh, and there was none softer than at the base of the throat.

Horrified, Toad grabbed the stake and did the very thing he should not have done; he ripped it out, and shrieked. Fargo bucked upwards as blood sprayed on his hair and shoulders. Grub was still looking at Spack and Maxine and had not realized what had happened until Toad shrieked. Bleating in surprise, he grabbed for his revolver.

Fargo's fingers found it first. A quick flick, and Fargo had the Remington in his hand. He jammed the muzzle against Grub's side and fired. . . .

THE

TRAILSMAN

#288

GILA RIVER
DRY-GULCHERS

by

Jon Sharpe

A SIGNET BOOK

SIGNET
Published by New American Library, a division of
Penguin Group (USA) Inc., 375 Hudson Street,
New York, New York 10014, USA
Penguin Group (Canada), 90 Eglinton Avenue East, Suite 700, Toronto,
Ontario M4P 2Y3, Canada (a division of Pearson Penguin Canada Inc.)
Penguin Books Ltd., 80 Strand, London WC2R 0RL, England
Penguin Ireland, 25 St. Stephen's Green, Dublin 2,
Ireland (a division of Penguin Books Ltd.)
Penguin Group (Australia), 250 Camberwell Road, Camberwell, Victoria 3124,
Australia (a division of Pearson Australia Group Pty. Ltd.)
Penguin Books India Pvt. Ltd., 11 Community Centre, Panchsheel Park,
New Delhi - 110 017, India
Penguin Group (NZ), cnr Airborne and Rosedale Roads, Albany,
Auckland 1310, New Zealand (a division of Pearson New Zealand Ltd.)
Penguin Books (South Africa) (Pty.) Ltd., 24 Sturdee Avenue,
Rosebank, Johannesburg 2196, South Africa

Penguin Books Ltd., Registered Offices:
80 Strand, London WC2R 0RL, England

First published by Signet, an imprint of New American Library,
a division of Penguin Group (USA) Inc.

First Printing, October 2005
10 9 8 7 6 5 4 3 2 1

The first chapter of this book previously appeared in *California Camel Corps,*
the two hundred eighty-seventh volume in this series.

The Trailsman

Beginnings . . . they bend the tree and they
mark the man. Skye Fargo was born when
he was eighteen. Terror was his midwife,
vengeance his first cry. Killing spawned Skye
Fargo, ruthless, cold-blooded murder. Out of
the acrid smoke of gunpowder still hanging
in the air, he rose, cried out a promise never
forgotten.

The Trailsman they began to call him all
across the West: searcher, scout, hunter, the
man who could see where others only
looked, his skills for hire but not his soul, the
man who lived each day to the fullest, yet
trailed each tomorrow. Skye Fargo, the
Trailsman, the seeker who could take the
wildness of a land and the wanting of a
woman and make them his own.

The sun-baked Gila Mountains, 1861—
where silver bred greed,
and lust bred bloodshed.

1

The heat could kill. One hundred and fifteen degrees in the shade, and there was precious little shade.

To the big man in buckskins winding through the Gila Mountains it was like being baked alive. But his whipcord body absorbed the blistering heat and did not wither. In him the sun had met its match. He was the man others had taken to calling the Trailsman.

Skye Fargo was taller than most and had shoulders so broad that every woman he met yearned to cling to them. His uncommonly handsome face was framed by a short-trimmed beard and a white hat, now nearly brown with dust. A red bandanna was knotted around his neck. But his most striking aspect was his eyes. As blue as a high-country lake, they were the windows to a soul as tough as the land around him. Even tougher, when he had to be. And he might have to be soon.

For the past hour Fargo had been aware of faint sounds behind him. Not faint due to distance but faint because whoever was making the sounds was trying not to let their presence be known. He was being stalked. Since it was extremely unlikely that anyone with friendly intentions would stalk him, he rode with his right hand on the well-worn grips of his Colt and his body half-twisted so that he always had an eye on the winding ribbon of a trail behind him.

Fargo did not know who it was, except that there was more than one. He did know the stalkers were not Apaches. No self-respecting warrior would be so noisy. The Apache moved as silently as a whisper and killed with no forewarning. Whoever was back there had to be white, and not overly bright whites, at that.

Fargo did not stop to wait nor did he bother to circle around and come up on them from behind. They would make their move when they were ready, and unknown to them, he would be prepared. If he was wrong, if they were not up to no good, all the better. But if there was one lesson he had learned in his years roaming the wilds, it was to regard strangers as enemies until they proved they were friendly.

A bead of sweat trickled from under his hat and left a moist mark down his right cheek. Flicking out his tongue, Fargo licked the drop off before it reached his chin. Such a tiny drop of moisture, yet it was welcome relief to his parched throat. He would be glad when he reached the Gila River, and his destination.

The letter that had brought Fargo to this godforsaken part of the desert Southwest was tucked in his saddlebags. He saw it again in his mind's eye, the neatly penned lines by Clarice Hammond begging him to come help her family find their father. "Implored" was the word Miss Hammond used. Her impeccable grammar suggested to Fargo that she was a lady of breeding and learning. Not exactly the kind of woman he would expect to find in a hell hole like Gila Bend.

The town sprang to life four years ago when a prospector stumbled on a vein of silver. Before you could say lickety-split, hundreds of folks who worshiped at the altar of human greed had turned a strip of land along the Gila River into Gila Bend, yet another boom town that would go bust the moment the ore ran out. Fargo had seen more than his share of such towns and they were always the same: wild, woolly, and deadly for those who were not quick with a gun or quicker with their wits.

Fargo was not one to brag, but he was both. Otherwise he would not have survived as long as had. He never sought trouble, but neither did he run from it when it came his way—as those behind him were about to learn.

In another half an hour Fargo came to where the trail widened near the base of a giant stone slab. Reining up in the slab's shadow, he stiffly dismounted, then stretched. The Ovaro was layered with sweat and wearily hung its head. "We don't have far to go, boy," he assured it. "Tonight you'll rest in a stable and eat your fill of oats."

The mention of food, even if for his horse, made Fargo's stomach rumble. He had been living on pieces of pemmican and jerky for the past week, and he was looking forward to a thick, juicy steak with all the trimmings.

Then hooves clattered, and Fargo put all thoughts of steak from his mind and turned to confront the three men who were riding toward him with smiles plastered on their grime-streaked faces. He pretended to be just as sociable and smiled back. "Howdy, gents." But his thumb was hooked in his gun belt close to his Colt, and his rifle was within easy reach in his saddle scabbard.

The trio were cut from the same coarse cloth. Their clothes were as dirty as they were, their boots badly scuffed. Two sported unkempt beards. The third, the rider in the lead, was a small man with ferret features and ferret eyes and stubble dotting his ferret chin. He was the dangerous one, the one whose eyes gleamed with craftiness. The one most likely to shoot Fargo in the back if Fargo was fool enough to turn it to him.

"Howdy, there, friend," the ferret declared. "You must be bound for Gila Bend, the same as us."

"Must be," Fargo said. Inwardly he smiled when all three glanced at his right hand, and the Colt.

The ferret and his companions reined up and the ferret took off his short-brimmed hat and wiped his brow with a dusty sleeve. "Folks hereabouts call me Spack. These are my pards, Grub and Toad."

Fargo went on smiling but did not tell them his name as they were waiting for him to do.

"Well," Spack said amiably. He replaced his hat and tugged on the brim. "I reckon I can't blame you for not tellin' us who you are, what with all the killin's and such the past month and a half."

"Been a lot, has there?" Fargo asked.

"Mister, you wouldn't believe it," Spack said. "Nineteen people have gone missin' and eleven others have been found murdered. It's gettin' so a decent hombre can't go anywhere unless he's got eyes in the back of his head."

"I know the feeling," Fargo responded dryly.

Spack gazed at the surrounding range. The Gila Mountains were low and barren, the highest peak not much over three thousand feet high. Compared to the Rockies they were more like hills, but they were as stark and rugged as their much higher kin, and certain death to the unwary. "This is a hard land."

"Hard enough," Fargo agreed. The other two were slowly moving their mounts to either side while trying not to be obvious about it. Amateurs, he thought with scorn, and they would get what they had coming.

Spack went on talking, trying to lull him into making a mistake. "They say most of the people who went missin' were taken by the Renegade."

"Who?"

"That's what they call him. The Renegade. No one has ever laid eyes on him but they reckon he's an Apache. Who else would carve 'em up so?"

"You've lost me," Fargo admitted.

"The bodies that have been found," Spack said. "Most of 'em were cut up somethin' awful. Noses gone, ears chopped off, tongues cut out, that sort of

4

thing." He scowled. "Everyone knows how Apaches like to whittle on whites."

"But why do they think it's just one?" With the tally at thirty, Fargo was inclined to think a war party was to blame.

" 'Cause tracks have been found near some of the bodies," Spack related. "Moccasin prints. Apache moccasins. And only one set."

"Which Apache tribe?" Fargo inquired. No two tribes made their moccasins exactly alike. An experienced tracker could always tell the difference. "Chiricahuas? Or the Mimbres?"

"How would I know? And who the hell cares? Redskins are redskins. We'd all be better off if every last one of the stinkin' heathens was six feet under."

"That's right," the one called Grub said. "It was Apaches killed my brother. Tied him upside down to a fence post, they did, and baked his brains."

"They don't like having their territory invaded," Fargo remarked.

"Invaded?" Spack snorted. "Whose side are you on, anyhow? So what if they were here before us? We're here now, and it's us or them who has to go away and it sure as hell won't be us."

"I hear that," Grub said gruffly.

Toad had not said a word. He was too busy cleaning out his left ear with his little finger. He wiped the wax off on his pants, then commented, "These parts aren't safe, no sir. It'd be smart if you rode with us."

Spack shot him a nasty look, as if Spack had wanted to make the offer himself, then smiled his oily smile. "Toad has a point. If you don't mind the company, you're welcome to tag along with us for protection."

"That's decent of you," Fargo said, trying not to laugh. "But I can manage on my own."

"Are you sure, friend?" Spack asked. "Extra guns in Apache country can come in mighty handy."

Fargo had no intention of riding with them just so they could fill him with lead at the first opportunity. Then again, it wouldn't do to have them go on stalking him, either. It made more sense to stick close so he could keep an eye on them. "You've changed my mind. I'll tag along after all."

"Smart man," Spack said by way of false praise. "You won't regret it. We're bound to make it to town in one piece." When Fargo just stood there, he asked, "What are you waitin' on?"

"My horse needs some rest," Fargo explained. "Go on ahead if you want. I'll catch up."

Spack did not like it but he forced a grin and a nod. "Whatever you want, mister. We'll be takin' our sweet time so there's no need to rush." Touching his hat brim, he clucked to his buttermilk.

Fargo watched the trio wind on down the mountain until they were out of sight. Mounting, he left the trail, picking his way with care through boulders and scrub brush until he was fifty yards out. Then he reined to the southwest. Soon he had caught up to the cutthroats and was paralleling them with them none the wiser.

They thought they had pulled the wool over his eyes. Joking and laughing, they never once gazed in Fargo's direction. Half a mile further on the trail narrowed, passing between two boulders the size of buffalo. Spack reined up. The three climbed down, and Spack had Grub stand behind one boulder and Toad behind the other with their rifles in hand.

Fargo reached for his Henry but let go of it without sliding it out. He squinted up at the burning sun, then at the three hardcases who were waiting for him to come along the trail so they could dry-gulch him, and he grinned. It would be an hour or more before they grew impatient and one of them rode back to see what had happened to him. An hour or more of the sweltering inferno. Chuckling, Fargo rode on, and when he had gone far enough to be safe, he returned to the trail and continued on his way.

Heat rose off the ground in unrelenting waves. The air itself was hot, and breathing it was like breathing fire. Fargo would just as soon be up in the Tetons at that time of year, but he could use the three hundred dollars Clarice Hammond was offering for his services. He had lost nearly every cent he had in a poker game a few weeks before.

Fargo thought again of her letter, and her missing father. He wondered if her father had fallen prey to the Renegade. If so, tracking down a lone Apache would take some doing. It posed more of a challenge than looking for the proverbial needle in a haystack, particulary since the needle would be out to kill.

The afternoon waxed and waned. The sun was nearing the western horizon when Fargo rounded a bend, and there, not far below, was a welcome sight.

Gila Bend, situated on the north side of the Gila River at a point where the river started to flow to the northwest along the edge of the Gila Mountains, was a motley collection of frame buildings and false fronts sprinkled with cabins and tents. Very few people were braving the heat but that would change once the sun went down.

The Ovaro quickened its pace without being prodded. The trail came out on flatland a quarter of a mile southeast of town. Fargo reined toward the river. At that time of year it was more akin to a creek but his throat didn't care. Water was water, and he lay on his belly and drank in great gulps, the Ovaro at his side. Smacking his lips, Fargo sat up and removed his hat and his bandanna. He dipped the bandanna in the river, wrung it out, and wiped the dust from his face and neck. A wonderful feeling of coolness spread over him but it was short-lived. Soon he was back in the saddle.

The sun was half gone when Fargo reached Gila

Bend. Long shadows cast the buildings in preternatural twilight. As he predicted, more people were moving about, a surprising number of them women. Or maybe not so surprising. Where there were riches to be made there were fallen doves out to separate the men who earned the riches from their money.

The grandest of the buildings was the Gila Hotel. By St. Louis or Kansas City standards it was second-rate, but it was the only building in town three stories high, and one of the few with glass in the windows. Four of five rocking chairs on a newly built boardwalk were occupied by ladies in bright dresses who brazenly regarded Fargo as a butcher might a fresh haunch of meat.

The fifth chair was filled by a gray-haired gentleman in a suit who arched a graying eyebrow and said, "What have we here? Another sheep to the slaughter. Another lamb to be fleeced."

"How's that?" Fargo asked, adjusting the saddle-bags he had thrown over his left shoulder. In his right hand was the Henry.

"Hold on to your poke or you won't have it long," the oldster warned. "If it's not a long-legged female who will get her hooks into you, it will be a cardsharp or a pickpocket."

"I don't fleece easy," Fargo said, "and I take it you have your poke."

The old man laughed. "Tricking someone my age takes some doing. But I take back what I said. It's plain as the wart on my nose that you're no green-horn." He offered a bony hand. "Fenton Wilson, at your service. I own this hotel."

"You?" Fargo could not keep the mild surprise out of his voice.

"What? I have too many gray hairs? Or should I be off in the mountains, risking life and limb for a paltry handful of rocks?" Fenton shook his head. "That's not for me, thank you very much. There are smart ways to make a living and there are dumb ways to make a living and if I haven't learned the difference at my age, take me and put me out of my misery."

Fargo shook. Wilson's skin reminded him of old leather but there was genuine warmth in the man's shake and in his expression. "I need a room."

"Would that I had one," Fenton said. "Mine have all been full every night ever since I had the place built."

"I was told there's one reserved in my name," Fargo said, and told the old-timer who he was.

Wilson blinked, then said, "Well, now." Slowly rising, he gestured for Fargo to go in ahead of him. "As a matter of fact, there is. Been holding it for weeks now." He looked Fargo up and down. "So you're him? The one they write about? Daniel Boone and Kit Carson rolled into one?"

"I'm just me," Fargo said. At moments like this he wished he could get his hands on the hacks who churned out story after story about every frontiersman of note, tales as tall as any ever told by a mountain man. The West was exciting news to the millions back East who lived drab lives but hankered after adventure, and the monthlies and the newspapers did their best to feed the demand.

The lobby was a haven for those not yet ready to brave the lingering heat of the fading day. Some sat, more stood, all chatting or reading or otherwise whiling away their time until the sun went down.

Fenton Wilson led Fargo to a counter near a flight of stairs and pushed a register toward him. "An X will do if you can't write."

Fargo signed his full name and was given the key to room 303. "It's on the third floor, toward the back. The Hammonds have six rooms, counting yours."

"Why so many?" Fargo wondered. Clarice Hammond had mentioned her family in the letter but had not said how many were with her.

"They wanted a suite and it's the best I could do,"

Fenton said. "One room for the mother, Janet, one room for each of the two daughters, Clarice and Millicent, a room for each of the brothers, Frank and Dexter, and a room for you."

"Are they up there now?" The sooner Fargo looked them up, the sooner he got his hands on the three hundred dollars.

"I don't believe so, no," Fenton replied. "They went out about half an hour ago. Down to Maxine's, if I recollect correctly, for supper. They eat early, those Hammonds. Comes from being from New Jersey, I suppose."

Fargo leaned his elbows on the counter. "What can you tell me about the father? They've hired me to try and find him."

"I know," Fenton said. Bending forward, he lowered his voice. "If you ask me, son, you've come all this way for nothing. As sure as I'm standing here, that jackass went and got himself killed. The only thing left to find of Desmond Hammond are his bones, and that's only if the scavengers have left any."

"How long has he been missing?"

"Let's see now. It'll be two months come the end of this week. He went off into the mountains on one of his many trips to find silver and never came back."

Fargo let out a sigh. He agreed with Fenton. After two months there was no hope in hell the father was still alive. It was too bad Clarice failed to mention it in her letter. Fenton was right about something else; he had come all this way for nothing. "Where do I find Maxine's?"

"Take a right out the door and go two blocks," Wilson said. "You can't miss it. Your nose will think it's in heaven." He paused. "But if you want to clean up first, I've got a tub in the back. I charge most folks a dollar for a bath but you can have one for free."

"Why so generous?" Fargo wanted to know.

Fenton Wilson shrugged. "I don't know. I reckon

I've taken a shine to you, and I don't take a shine to many." He acted embarrassed by the admission. "So what do you say?" he gruffly demanded. "Do you want the bath or not?"

Fargo was hungry enough to eat a buffalo, but he was more than a little whiffy from the long ride. It would not do to meet Clarice Hammond smelling like the south end of a northbound horse. "I'm obliged."

"Don't make a mountain out of an anthill of kindness."

Fargo placed the Henry and his saddlebags on the counter. "Can you have these taken up to my room?"

"Consider it done." Fenton picked up a bell and rang it. Within seconds a cherubic youngster materialized at Fargo's elbow.

"Yes, sir, Mr. Wilson, sir."

"Donny, this gentleman is to be treated to a bath on the house, and I—" Fenton abruptly stopped. "What's the matter with you, boy? Why is your mouth hanging open like that?"

"Did you say he gets his bath for free?" Donny was incredulous.

"Another smart-aleck remark like that and you'll be sweeping horse droppings for a living," Fenton warned. "Yes, I said for free, and what of it? You're to tend to the water personally and supply him with a towel and a bar of lye soap. Understood?"

"Yes, sir," Donny responded, but he still sounded as if he could not credit his ears. To Fargo he said, "This way, sir, if you please." He hustled past the counter and down a narrow hall to a door at the back. Working the latch, he stepped aside. "After you, sir."

Fargo entered. In addition to the tub there was a bench for his clothes and a small open window high in the rear wall. He turned, and found the youngster studying him as if he were a form of life the boy had never set eyes on before. "What?"

"Are you God Almighty, sir?"

"Are you drunk, boy?" Fargo rejoined.

"Oh, no, sir," Donny took him seriously. "My ma would take a switch to me if I so much as sniffed a glass of beer."

"I've been asked some dumb questions but that takes the prize. Next you'll want to know if silver grows on trees."

Donny smiled self-consciously. "I didn't mean it like that, sir. It's just that Mr. Wilson never does anything for free. *Never*," he stressed. "You must be awful special for him to treat you like this."

"I scout and track for a living," Fargo said. "Nothing special there." He also spent a lot of time at card tables and had been known to tip a bottle or three when he had time on his hands.

"Maybe so," Donny said. "But it's mighty strange Mr. Wilson is being so kind. He still has the first dollar he ever made. He told me so."

Fargo took off his hat and hung it on a peg. "There's always more to people than we think there is."

"Maybe so," Donny repeated, "but if I didn't know I was awake, I'd think I was dreaming."

It took seven trips for the boy to fill the tub, toting two full buckets of piping hot water from the kitchen each trip. The room became steamy.

Fargo waited for the last bucket to be poured, then slid a small roll of bills from his pocket and peeled off a five. "My horse is the Ovaro out front at the hitch rail. Take him to the livery and put him up for the night. I saw a sign that says it's two dollars so you give the liveryman the five and keep the three for yourself."

Donny's lower jaw had a habit of dropping like a trapdoor. "All *three*, sir? I can bring you the change if you want."

"All three," Fargo said. He had been the boy's age once, and hardly ever had fifty cents to his name. "But you have to go back to the livery later and make sure the liveryman has my Ovaro tucked away nice and cozy. Do we have a deal?"

"Mister, for three dollars I'd go after the Renegade with my slingshot," Donny declared, holding the bill as if it were the Holy Grail. "Anything you want, you just give a holler."

"I could use a towel and that bar of soap," Fargo reminded him, and the boy lit out of there like his britches were on fire. Donny was back in three shakes of a mule's tail and then whisked out again to tend to the Ovaro.

Fargo unbuckled his gun belt and placed it on the bench at arm's length from the tub. He stripped off his boots, shirt and pants, placing them beside it. He was about to shed his socks when he heard the door open. "Donny, that you?" he asked, glancing over his shoulder.

"Not hardly," Spack said as he, Grub and Toad sauntered in. "Remember us? We've been lookin' for you, you coyote."

2

Fargo had heard of being caught with one's pants down but never with one's pants off. The Colt was just out of reach. He started to sidle toward the bench and Spack smirked and placed a hand on the Remington at his waist.

"That wasn't very friendly of you."

"Is something wrong?" Fargo asked as innocently as he could. They had halted just inside the door and were eyeing him like wolves sizing up prey. He still had the Toothpick in its ankle sheath, but a knife against three pistols was a surefire invitation to an early grave.

"Oh, we just wondered where you got to, is all," Spack said with more than a hint of malice. "There we were, waitin' for you to catch up, and you never did."

Fargo shrugged. "I came another way. And I don't see where what I do is any of your business." He was calling their bluff, which was risky. But he could not see them gunning him down there in the hotel. People would come running. There would be too many witnesses.

"You're right," Spack said. "I reckon it isn't. But the least you could have done was let us know."

"You looked me up just to tell me that?" Fargo suspected there had to be more to it, but what, exactly, he couldn't say.

Spack smiled his fake smile. "We just wanted to be sure you made it safe and sound, is all. For all we knew, the Renegade turned you into maggot bait."

"How thoughtful of you," Fargo played his part. "Now why don't you gents mosey along and leave a man to his bath."

"Sure, sure," Spack said, and motioned at his partners, who sullenly withdrew. As Spack was going out he paused. "Gila Bend ain't all that big a town. We'll meet again, mister."

A threat, if ever Fargo heard one. He crossed to the door and threw the bolt so no one else could walk in on him. Then he climbed in the tub and eased down into the hot water, luxuriating in the feeling. Leaning back, he closed his eyes, and before he could stop himself, he was asleep.

A sound awakened him. Fargo sat up, sloshing the water, and looked around in mild confusion. The room was dark. Night had fallen and a few stars were visible out the high window.

The door shook to a loud thump. "Fargo?" Fenton Wilson bawled. "Are you alive in there? It's been over an hour! How long do you need to scrub yourself clean? I've got other folks who would like to use that tub."

"Be out in a minute," Fargo replied. The ends of his fingers had that shriveled look they always got when they were in water too long. He groped for the lye soap and began washing. He was in a hurry to get out, not so much on account of the other hotel patrons as the water was now almost cold. He scrubbed his face, then ran the bar over his hair and lathered his head. Taking a deep breath, he held it and sank under the water. Slowly rising, he carefully climbed out.

A brisk toweling, and Fargo was almost done. He

dressed, strapped on the Colt, placed his hat on his head, retied his bandanna, and was ready. Throwing the bolt, he took a step, and stopped.

"About damn time, you bath hog."

Nine people were lined up awaiting their turn. The first was an exceedingly plump woman who bestowed a withering look and shouldered past him like an angry she-bull.

"Out of my way."

"Sorry, ma'am," Fargo said, but she didn't hear him for the slamming of the door. He touched his hat brim to the others and made his way down the hall to the lobby, which was now practically deserted. Fenton Wilson was tending the front desk.

Fargo went over. "I fell asleep."

"I figured as much," the hotel owner said with a chortle. "Don't fret yourself. The ones who were waiting always need a bath before they go out at night. It's a powerful waste of water, if you ask me. Who ever heard of taking a bath a day?" He inserted a letter into a slot. "Besides, it makes a lot of extra work for me and the staff. For two bits I'd tell them to go jump in the Gila River."

Fargo liked the old cuss. "Refresh my memory. You did say Maxine's is two blocks down on the right?"

"Unless she's up and moved it when I wasn't looking," Fenton cracked. "But you might want to hold off on the food. While you were giving Miss Fitzgerald and the rest of the bath-a-day crowd conniptions, the Hammonds came back. They're up in their rooms."

Fargo weighed his choices and was persuaded by his rumbling stomach to choose the first. "I'll see them after. Did you tell them I was here?"

"Nope. I'm a firm believer in keeping my mouth shut unless I'm asked to open it. Better for the digestion."

Again Fargo's stomach growled, and this time Wilson heard.

"You'd best skedaddle before you keel over from starvation. I charge extra for taking up floor space."

Fargo was halfway to the entrance when he thought to ask, "Did your boy get my horse to the livery?"

"Donny? He's no relation of mine," Fenton said, misunderstanding. "He's one of five urchins who work for me. And come to think of it, I haven't seen him since I sent him to prepare your bath." He gazed around the lobby. "Now where in blazes could he have gotten to? It's not like him to disappear."

Fargo was out the door before Fenton stopped speaking. Instead of turning right to go to the restaurant, he turned left toward the livery. Donny had not struck him as the irresponsible sort. The boy should have been back by now.

Two steps into the stable Fargo spied the Ovaro in a stall. His saddle and saddle blanket had been stripped and draped over the side. The Ovaro was munching on oats, as content as could be.

Fargo went back out. He was worse than a biddy hen, the way he worried over nothing. It came from spending so much of his time on the frontier, where someone out to do him harm might be lurking behind any boulder or tree. It ingrained the habit of looking for trouble where there wasn't any.

Chuckling to himself, Fargo bent his steps to Maxine's. A sign proclaimed to the world that it was *the finest eatery west of the Pecos. Our specialty is pie, fresh out of the oven.*

The place was packed. If there was another restaurant in Gila Bend, you wouldn't know it from the wall-to-wall humanity that filled every table to overflowing. Fargo walked down an aisle between long tables and started up the next, searching for a space to cram into.

"Seats sure are hard to come by at times."

The voice was female and friendly. Fargo turned to find a stunning redhead in a blue dress and a yellow apron holding a coffeepot in one hand while balancing a tray laden with plates and bowls in the other. "I could always sit in a corner."

"Nonsense. Follow me." Without waiting for a reply, the redhead hurried down the aisle to a door at the rear and shouldered through it into a large, hot kitchen. A burly bald man in an apron was at the stove, overseeing four sizzling pans and a couple of boiling pots. She bobbed her chin at a small table to one side. "Will that do?"

"It will do fine," Fargo said. "So long as it doesn't get you in hot water with the boss."

The redhead smiled. She had lovely green eyes and an aquiline nose and lips as full and red as ripe cherries. "I wouldn't worry there. I'm Maxine. Maxine Walters."

"Pleased to meet you." Fargo introduced himself, making no attempt to hide his admiration for her marvelous figure. She had an ample bosom, a waist he could put both hands around, and legs that seemed to go on forever.

"So I notice," Maxine responded, but she was not upset. To the contrary, she grinned as if pleased.

The bald man had turned from the stove. "What's this, Max? Since when do we let customers in the kitchen?"

"We?" Max said. "I can have anyone back here I want. Mr. Fargo is using the table we normally eat at." She held out a chair for Fargo to sit in, then gave him a one-sheet menu. "Whatever you want is on the house."

Fargo glanced at her over the menu. First Fenton gave him a free bath, now this. "If this is what happens when I take a bath, I'll take them more often."

Maxine had a ravishing smile. "I won't deny you're better looking than most but it's not that. You did my son a kindness and for that I'm very grateful."

"Your son?" Fargo repeated, and wanted to slap

himself. "Oh. You mean Donny? He told you about the tip?"

"He rushed in here on his way back from the stable," Maxine said. "I'd never seen him so excited. It's the largest tip anyone has ever given him."

"He's a good boy," Fargo said to be polite.

"That he is," Maxine said with undisguised pride. "The apple of my eye. It's been rough having to raise him all by my lonesome and sometimes I worry I'm not doing as much as I should. It was his idea to get a job to help me out."

"You're in need of money?" Fargo nodded toward the packed dining room. "Seems to me you're making it hand over fist."

"Things are never as they seem." Maxine opened her mouth to say more but just then the bald cook called her name.

"I've got four more orders ready to go. Do you want me to take them or should I let the food get cold?"

"You must excuse Sam," Maxine said. "He tends to think he's a mother hen and I'm a baby chick." She swirled away. "I'll be back in a few minutes for your order."

The menu offered over a dozen dishes, among them chicken soup, dumplings, beef stew, Boston baked beans and pork, and macaroni. At the very bottom was steak and potatoes. Fargo smacked his lips in anticipation just as a shadow fell across him. Thinking it was Maxine Walters, he lowered the menu.

"I don't know what you're up to, mister," Sam said harshly, "but I'm telling you here and now to stay away from Max."

It was Fargo's day for being put upon, and he did not like it. He did not like it one bit. "And if I don't?"

"Then you're dumber than an anvil and deserve what you get," Sam snapped. "Don't let me see you back here again, or anywhere near her, for that matter." He glanced at the door to the dining room, then hurried to the stove.

Fargo did not say anything about Sam when Maxine returned. He was conscious of Sam's cold stares but they did not spoil his enjoyment of the meal. The steak was juicy and succulent, and he chewed each piece with relish. The potatoes were drowning in butter, the bread half an inch thick. He washed it all down with several cups of delicious coffee. He had just pushed back his plate and was leaning back in his chair when Maxine floated over.

"I trust it was to your liking?"

"I never tasted better," Fargo said.

"You're too kind, but there are restaurants in places like New Orleans and New York City that make our food seem like hog swill."

Fargo noticed Sam watching from over by the stove. "Are you always so hard on yourself?"

"I suppose I am," Maxine admitted. "My confidence isn't all it should be. That comes from having a husband walk out on me and head for Oregon with a dance hall floozy who—" She abruptly stopped, and blushed.

"Any man who would leave you is a jackass," Fargo bluntly declared. "You have a lot to be proud about. Your son. Making a go of it on your own. Owning your own business."

"Oh, the restaurant isn't mine," Max revealed. "Fenton Wilson is the owner, I just run it for him."

"Do tell," Fargo said. Wilson never mentioned it to him, but then again, why should he?

"I earn fifty cents an hour," Maxine said. "Ten hour days, seven days a week," she added rather regretfully. "Except for two days each month I get off."

Fargo did the math in his head. That was a hundred and forty dollars a month, about the same as a bank clerk. "A lot of people don't make half as much as you do," he remarked. Cowboys, for instance, typically earned anywhere from forty to sixty dollars a month. A sheriff's deputy made only seventy-five.

"It's more than fair," Maxine conceded, "but my husband saddled me with a lot of debts I have to pay off before I can keep much of my pay for myself. That's why Donny took the job at the hotel. To help me out."

Fargo pulled out his small roll of bills. "I'm grateful for the meal but I wouldn't feel right if I didn't pay." Especially after learning what he had just learned. "How much do I owe you?"

Maxine locked her lovely green eyes on his. "You don't need to. It's the least I can do for you being so kind to Donny."

"There are other things," Fargo said, and when she blushed anew, he quickly added, "Such as letting me treat you to a meal on one of your days off. Or whatever else you might like to do."

"Why, Mr. Fargo, am I to gather you are asking me out?" Maxine playfully bantered.

"Friend to friend," Fargo enlightened her. "No strings. I'm not up to no good. I'd just enjoy your company."

Maxine was quiet for a bit. Then she softly said, "I would be delighted to go out with you. As a matter of fact, my next day off is tomorrow. So if you wanted, you could pick me up at the Adams boardinghouse on First Street, say, about six?"

"I'll be there." Fargo paid and added an extra dollar for her, then pocketed the few he had left. The noisy dining room was still crammed wall to wall. The street, too, bustled with activity now that the sun had relinquished the heavens to the stars and a sliver of silvery moon. A stiff breeze out of the northwest had dispelled much of the lingering heat.

As with most boomtowns, Gila Bend boasted a motley assortment of citizens. Prospectors, gamblers, doves, mule skinners, clerks, cowboys and others were enjoying the rowdy nightlife for which boomtowns were noted.

Fargo had not gone a block when a petite brunette in a dress two sizes too small sashayed out of the shadows and wriggled her hips invitingly.

"What's your rush, handsome? Five dollars and I'm yours for an hour, thirty dollars and I'm yours for the night."

"I just spent my last fifty cents," Fargo fibbed. Some soiled doves became downright mad when a man refused their amorous advances.

"Too bad," the brunette said teasingly. "Something tells me you'd treat a girl to a night she wouldn't soon forget." With a wistful sigh she touched his chin and was gone, melting into the stream of humanity.

The hotel lobby was empty save for Fenton, who was reading a newspaper. Fargo slipped by him without being noticed and padded lightly up the stairs to the third floor. He slid the key into the lock to 303 and it opened with a slight rasp. His saddlebags were on the dresser, his rifle was propped in a corner. He started to shut the door but fingers curled around it and someone applied pressure from the other side. Slender fingers, with strawberry-red fingernails. He swung the door wide open.

The woman who stood there was older than Fargo by about twenty years but she was remarkably well preserved. Sandy hair hung low over delicate arched eyebrows. Her face was oval and without blemish, her lips too thin but her eyes an alluring shade of violet. She wore a dress cut extraordinarily low across her bosom. In her left hand was a half-empty glass of whiskey. "So you're him? The famous scout my daughter sent for?"

"Janet Hammond," Fargo guessed.

"You know me?" Janet dismissed her own question with a wave of her other hand. "Never mind. The important thing is that at last you're here and we can get this fiasco over with."

"Fiasco?" Fargo said. "I was told your husband has gone missing."

"Missing, hell. The idiot is dead by now, and it serves him right for traipsing off into the mountains after rainbows." Janet giggled and took a long sip, her eyes roving up and down Fargo's frame. "I was going downstairs for a fresh bottle and saw you unlock your door."

"You don't seem very broken up by your husband's disappearance," Fargo mentioned, trying to gauge her reaction.

Janet Hammond snickered and took another sip. "I have no sympathy for fools and my husband was a fool from the day he was born. He was so certain he would strike it rich! He dragged us all the way here from New Jersey. Why I came I will never know." She finished her drink in a single gulp, then stared morosely at the empty glass. "Damn."

"Is Clarice here? I need to talk to her."

Janet nodded. "She's in her room with the rest of the nitwits. Tell you what. Why don't you take me over to the saloon for an hour or so; then you can meet with them and talk over how best to find my husband's mortal remains."

Fargo was puzzled. It was considered poor taste for any decent woman to ever set foot in an establishment that sold liquor. And her concern for her husband's welfare, to say nothing of her opinion of her own children, was hardly that of a devoted wife and loving mother. "I really should talk to Clarice."

Janet smiled seductively and ran a finger across his cheek. "Is it that you don't find me attractive? I'm not getting any younger, I know."

"You're married," Fargo said.

A stunned look came over her, and Janet Hammond took a step back. "Well, this is a surprise. From what

I've heard, you have the morals of an alley cat. Rumor has it you sleep with anything in petticoats."

"Rumor is often wrong," Fargo said curtly. No man liked to have his face rubbed in his dalliances. She was interested in one thing and one thing only, just like that dove earlier—only the dove was more honest about it. He started to walk past her. "Which room is your daughter in?"

"Touchy, aren't we?" Janet said mockingly, blocking his path. She leaned against him, her bosom warm on his chest, and cooed in a sultry tone, "Are you sure I can't change your mind?"

Fargo gave her both barrels. "We can do it right here in the hall and charge people to watch."

Janet grimaced as if she had been struck and took a step back, her lips a slit, her eyelids hooded. "I offer you a good time and you throw it in my face? Very well, Mr. High-and-Mighty. Follow me." She spun on a heel and stalked to 304. Without bothering to knock, she opened it and brusquely announced, "Your buckskin buffoon has arrived!"

"Mother!" a girlish voice exclaimed.

Smirking, Janet stood aside so Fargo could enter. She closed the door behind them and leaned against it, wagging her empty glass in small circles.

Two women were seated in chairs by the window. Two men were lounging on the bed. The women sat up, the men slid to their feet, all four regarding Fargo with keen interest. They took his measure while he was taking theirs.

The youngest of the women was not a day over twenty, if that. She had her mother's sandy hair but her features were more attractive and her body more shapely. The other woman was in her early twenties, Fargo reckoned, with raven hair cropped short and blue eyes much paler than his. Her skin was pale, too. She had pink lips cast in a perpetual quirk. They were not that alike, and yet there were enough similarities to show they were related.

The men were older although not by many years. Fargo guessed the oldest to be between twenty-five and thirty. They both had short crinkly brown hair, long noses, and protruding chins. If not for the age difference they could be twins.

"Mr. Fargo, thank you for coming!" the youngest woman said, and came forward to clasp his hand in hers. "I'm Clarice Hammond. This is my sister, Millicent. And these are my brothers, Frank and Dexter."

Fargo shook hands with the brothers and it was like shaking a pair of limp rags. Neither was all that enthusiastic about meeting him.

Clarice indicated the chair she had vacated. "Why don't you have a seat and we will get down to business? As I mentioned in my letter, our father has gone missing and we want you to find him."

Fargo stayed where he was. "You didn't tell me he's been missing for two months. If you had I wouldn't be here."

Taken aback, Clarice raised a hand to her throat. "Why would you say a thing like that?"

"Your father is long dead by now," Fargo gave it to her straight. "Hiring me to find him would be a waste of my time and your money."

"It's mine to waste as I see fit," Clarice said peevishly. "And I happen to believe my father is very much alive. I *know* it, as surely as I know you and I are standing here talking."

Janet Hammond made a sound reminiscent of a goose being strangled. "Please, daughter. Listen to the man. He agrees with me and nearly everyone else that Desmond's idiocy caught up with him. It's about time you admitted the truth so we can all get on with our lives."

"Don't start, Mother," Clarice said.

"It's sad, is all, seeing you delude yourself this way," Janet said. "I always gave you credit for being the smartest of the dunces."

Millicent rose from her chair. "We are not dunces, Mother. And I'll thank you not to insult us in the presence of company."

"Oh, please," Janet said, and focused on Fargo. "Talk some sense into them, will you? I've tried and tried, but what can you do when you're dealing with simpletons?" She tipped the glass to her mouth and then realized she had yet to refill it and swore under her breath. "Tell them there's not one reason in hell for you to risk life and limb searching for my buffoon of a husband. Tell them I've been right all along. Maybe it will sink into their thick skulls."

A tear trickled down Clarice's left cheek. Millicent had her fists clenched and was beet red. Frank and Dexter were carven statues.

They all looked at Fargo expectantly, and he surprised himself as much as he surprised them by saying, "Then again, why come all this way for nothing? I'll take the job." Only then did he wonder what in the world he was letting himself in for.

3

Half an hour later Fargo was back in his room. He had a lot to ponder.

Apparently, Desmond Hammond announced to his wife one day out of the blue that he was heading west to make his fortune, and off he went. He panned for gold for a short while in the Rockies west of Denver but the long hours and the cold water were not to his liking, so when he heard of the silver strike in the Gila Mountains, and how silver ore was just waiting to be plucked out of the ground, off he rushed to claim his share.

Janet Hammond was the one who told Fargo the story and the scorn in her voice was thick enough to cut with a blunt butter knife. "My husband always has been a bit of an idiot," she stated, right there in front of her children. "I've humored him as best I'm able but there are limits."

"Mother!" Millicent said.

Janet ignored her. "That was six months ago. I wrote him a few times asking him to come home but he refused. He insisted he would make a big strike. Then his weekly letters stopped coming. Not long after, I received one from Mr. Wilson informing me of Desmond's disappearance. I came right away, and these"—Janet encompassed her offspring with a gesture—"insisted on accompanying me. We hired locals to try and find him, to no avail. Desmond was secretive about his prospecting and never told anyone where he was searching." She gazed sadly into her empty glass. "Anyway, Clarice heard of you and decided to contact you on her own, and here you are, wasting your time and ours."

Ironically, Fargo felt the same. But he had agreed to help Clarice to spite her mother. He could at least find Desmond's mortal remains and put the family's worries to rest.

As for the family, Fargo was unsure what to make of them. Janet lived in a bottle, that much was certain, and had little love for her husband or her children. Clarice and Millicent seemed decent enough, although like most Easterners, they were as helpless as newborn babes when it came to the wilds of the West. The brothers were no better. Frank and Dexter had said very little the whole time Fargo was there. He had the impression they were afraid of their mother, and unlike their sisters, never stood up to her.

A strange family, the Hammonds, and here he was, getting mixed up with them. Fargo shook his head in annoyance at himself. He knew better. But that tear trickling down Clarice's cheek had done what no amount of persuasion could.

Sighing, Fargo was about to get undressed and turn in early when there came a light rap on his door. He opened it expecting to find one of the Hammonds but it was a boy about Donny's age. "What do you want?"

"Sorry, sir, but I was asked to give you a message," the boy recited. "Mrs. Walters would like to see you out back of the hotel."

"Out back?" Fargo wondered what Maxine wanted. Maybe she had snuck away from the restaurant for a bit and did not want Fenton Wilson to find out. "Lead the way." He stepped out and closed his door.

"You can take the back stairs down," the boy said, pointing. "I have to get back to work or Mr. Wilson will be mad."

"You work here?"

"Yes, sir. I just relieved Donny. My name is Abe." He skipped off toward the front stairs.

Fargo locked his door and went down the back. One of the hinges creaked as he stepped out into the night. Half an acre away stood another building. Between them grew dry grass and weeds. There were no lamps or lanterns and the only light came from several of the windows above. "Maxine?" he said, turning left and then right.

The blow to his head nearly buckled his knees. Instinctively, Fargo threw himself backward and grabbed for the door but another blow to his shoulder rendered his right arm completely numb. Staggering to one side, he shook his head to clear it and heard a sadistic laugh.

"You wouldn't listen. I warned you to stay away from her and you went and made a date for tomorrow."

Fargo's vision began to clear and he saw the burly cook from the restaurant, no longer wearing the apron and holding a stout club. "So it was you who sent the boy," he stalled. His shoulder was tingling and he could flex his fingers but he could not quite move his arm.

"I paid him fifty cents," Sam rasped. "He knows me so he never suspected a thing." Edging forward, he said, "Ever had every bone in your body busted?"

Fargo willed his right hand to stab for his Colt but a thousand prickling points of pain flared in his shoulder and his arm would not move as it should. Backing away, he fell into a crouch. "What will Maxine say when she finds out about this?" Not that he would tell her. He was still stalling.

"What does it matter?" Sam rejoined. "There's more going on here than you think. You'd be wise to pack up in the morning and head out."

"I have a job to do," Fargo said.

"Desmond Hammond?" Sam snorted. "So I've heard. All the more reason for me to beat the stuffing out of you."

"What's he to you?"

"Not a damn thing. And neither are you."

Fargo was braced for the rush. He ducked under a swing that would have caved in his skull and dodged another that came close to crushing his windpipe. Sidestepping, he tried moving his right arm but it rose only a few inches.

Sam raised the club overhead. "You're quick, I'll give you that, but you can't keep this up forever."

No, Fargo couldn't. Which was why he raised his left arm as if to block the blow, but then, before the club could sweep down, he kicked the cook in the knee.

Howling in pain, Sam skipped backward, favoring his left leg. "Damn you!" he roared. "Damn you to hell!"

"The thing about breaking bones," Fargo said, "is that it works both ways."

"I'll kill you! You hear me?" Sam fumed, and tried to charge but his hurt knee threw him off balance.

Twisting, Fargo felt the swish of air as the club flashed past his face. He kicked out again, connecting with the other knee.

A bellow of commingled pain and fury tore from the cook. Sam tried to retreat out of reach but his right leg gave way and he fell. Grimacing, he tossed his head from side to side, spittle flecking his lips. "You broke it! You broke my knee, you bastard!"

"I don't think so," Fargo said. He hadn't heard a

crack. Now, stepping in close, he flicked his foot again and sent the club flying into the dark. Then, raising both fists, he said grimly, "Whenever you're ready."

Sam blinked. A savage grin split his face. "I'll be damned. You're not going to pistol-whip me while I'm down?"

Fargo should. The man had it coming. But this would give him just as much satisfaction, if not more. "On your feet, you miserable son of a bitch."

The bald man slowly rose. He had a bull neck and thick shoulders and arms and knuckles the size of walnuts. "You just made a big mistake, mister. No one has ever taken me with their fists. Not ever."

"There's a first time for everything."

"I admire a gent with confidence," Sam said sarcastically, and waded in, limping but determined.

Holding his ground, Fargo countered a series of jabs. The cook was taking his measure. He let him. He was content to block and slip a dozen or so punches. Then Sam delivered an uppercut. Slipping aside, Fargo delivered one of his own. It lifted the cook onto his heels.

Fargo could have ended it then and there. A solid right would bring Sam crashing down. But it was too soon. Much too soon. He set himself, and when Sam recovered enough to wade in again, he slipped a left jab, feinted with his own left, and followed through with a right to the gut.

Doubling over, Sam gasped and wheezed and turned several shades of purple. His arms and shoulders were muscular but his belly was a water skin, or maybe, in his case, a beer or an ale skin, as soft as a pillow. "Going to stomp you!" he huffed. "Going to pound you into the dirt!"

Fargo said nothing. His actions would speak for him, and his next act, as Sam struggled to rise, was to dart in and clip him on the ear.

Yipping like a kicked cur, Sam thrashed wildly

about, one hand on his ear, the other on his stomach. When at length he stopped thrashing, he glared balefully up at Fargo and snarled through clenched teeth, "No one does this to me! You hear?"

The man was all bluster. Fargo had met his kind before—two-legged bulls who thought they were meaner and tougher than everyone else, and who had to learn the hard way that no matter how tough a man was, there was always someone tougher, always someone who could do to them as they enjoyed doing to others.

Sam got his hands under him and levered to his feet. His ear was bleeding and his jaw was discolored and he moved stiffly on account of his sore knees but he still had fight left in him. "No more taking it easy on you."

Fargo smiled grimly. On the frontier hardcases were a penny a dozen, and not one could make it through a fight without bragging about how he was going to do this, that, or the other. Fargo never bragged. Experience had taught him that talking a fierce fight was not the same as being a good fighter. In the end, skill always won out over boasts.

Sam came in again, swinging nonstop, a whirlwind of jabs, hooks, crosses and straight-arm blows. He was trying to batter Fargo down by sheer brute force and he soon discovered, as his shocked expression showed, the truth of the matter.

Fargo was stronger. Others had made the mistake of misjudging him. He was tall but he was not heavy. He had broad shoulders but they were not all that thick. So it was natural for big, beefy men to think he would be easy to beat. They failed to take into account the kind of life he led. Living in the wilds honed a man's reflexes to a razor's edge. Even more importantly, it forged his sinews into living steel. There wasn't an ounce of fat anywhere on Fargo's body. He was muscle, all muscle, compact and lean and as hard as flint.

Sam tried another uppercut and received two swift jabs to the ribs that elicited a wince. He threw an overhand only to have Fargo duck and slam a cross to the wind that staggered him. When Fargo did not exploit his advantage, the cook froze and blurted, "You're toying with me."

Fargo stayed silent.

"You're doing this to punish me," Sam said. "You want to hurt me bad for hurting you." He was sweating profusely and breathing so raggedly, he sucked in breaths between each word.

Again, Fargo did not respond.

"Damn you!" Sam puffed. "Damn you to hell! I'm only doing what I'm supposed to do!"

Despite himself, Fargo's interest perked. "What do you mean?"

"Nothing," Sam said much too quickly. "You have me so rattled I can't think straight." Suddenly he lowered his arms and stepped back. "No more. If you want to beat on me, go ahead. But I won't hit back."

Now it was Fargo who boiled with anger. "You giving up? Just like that?"

"I know when I'm licked. I don't have a chance in hell against you. As it is, I'll be bruised and sore for a month of Sundays and my ear will be as big as a cauliflower by morning." Sam started to turn.

"This isn't over," Fargo told him.

The cook froze and worriedly glanced at the back door to the hotel, evidently debating whether to try and reach it before Fargo reached him. "I meant what I said. I won't hit back."

"You're to let Maxine Walters be," Fargo said. "She's free to live her life as she pleases. That includes seeing anyone she wants."

"And if I don't?"

"We'll take up where we left off," Fargo vowed. And he meant it.

Sam made another peculiar comment. "What have I gotten myself into? It isn't worth it."

"What isn't?"

His puffy lips crooked in a lopsided smirk, Sam wagged a thick finger. "Oh, no, you don't. I've blabbed too much already. But take my word for it. I'm through." With that, he turned and hobbled off, glancing fearfully over a shoulder as if afraid Fargo would come after him.

Fargo didn't. He was trying to make sense of it all but the cook's remarks made no sense. He was about to go back in the hotel when the odor of liquor wafted to his nose. "How long have you been there?"

Janet Hammond was leaning against the back door exactly as she had leaned against her daughter's bedroom door earlier. In her right hand was her ever-present glass, only now it was three-fourths full. "That was something to behold!" she declared.

"You didn't answer my question."

"My goodness, aren't we in a mood?" the whiskey-soaked matriarch of the Hammond clan lightheartedly commented. "But for your information, I overheard the boy and you talking and followed the two of you down."

"Snooping," Fargo said, his estimation of her dropping several more notches. "Some men would slap you silly for that."

"But not you," Janet said with a mischievous grin. "You're not the kind to beat on a woman even when she deserves it."

"You don't know me," Fargo reminded her.

"Oh, please. I wasn't born yesterday. You have a good streak in you although you try hard to deny it. That's why you agreed to help my daughter. That, and you wanted to get back at me for being the bitch you think I am."

Fargo had to hand it to her. She had him figured out. "If you're not a bitch, you sure pretend real well."

Laughter tinkled from Janet's throat. "I pretend a lot of things. It helps me make it through the day. That, and this." Janet took a long swallow and smacked her lips. "If you were in my shoes you would do the same."

"I doubt it."

"Oh, do you, indeed?" Janet came closer and wagged the glass at him. "It just shows how much you don't know." Sadness came over her and she gazed miserably at the starry sky. "Do you have any idea what it's like to marry someone weaker than you? I don't mean just physically weaker. I mean someone mentally and emotionally weaker. A weakling in every sense of the word." She swallowed more whiskey. "Desmond was as weak as can be. He couldn't make a decision if his life depended on it. And he was always letting others step on him. Business associates. So-called friends. Anybody."

Fargo let her have her say.

"Why, one time, shortly after I married him, we were on our way to the theater and a couple of young men came up and were making lewd suggestions to me, and do you know what Desmond did?" Janet did not wait for an answer. "Nothing! Absolutely nothing! He let them insult me and never raised a finger. I was never so ashamed of anyone in my whole life."

"Ashamed of him for not defending you," Fargo said.

"No. Ashamed of myself for marrying him."

"Why did you, then?" Fargo asked.

"They say that love is blind and they are right. Especially when one is young and has no experience in matters of the heart. I was so in love with him that I was blind to his faults until well after we were man and wife. I've been stuck with him ever since."

"There's always divorce."

"Spoken like a man," Janet said in contempt. "Do you have any idea how hard it is to get one? And the stigma attached to the wife when it happens?" She took another swallow. "A woman is better off suffering in silence. Although I must confess, I have never been able to keep quiet when I've been wronged." Yet another swallow. "For decades I've endured a living hell."

Fargo wondered what it must have been like for Desmond Hammond, wed to a woman who thought he was less than a man and probably carped on his weakness ten times a day. But something didn't quite add up. "You say he never made decisions. But your daughter said it was his idea to come west."

"Believe me, nothing ever surprised me more. I thought he was joking at first. When I realized he wasn't, I went along with his foolishness to encourage him to be more manly. I let him come. The one time he stood on his own two feet, and look at what it's brought me? I'm a widow." Janet emptied the glass and made as if to throw it against the hotel but lowered her arm. "Desmond would still be alive if I had told him what I really thought about his ridiculous venture."

"We don't know he's dead."

"Now who is pretending? Let's not delude ourselves. Clarice and the others are clutching at a straw. They refuse to accept the truth. You and I are more mature."

"There's always a chance," Fargo said even though he did not believe it himself. "Clarice told me he took two pack animals and plenty of provisions. Enough to last him weeks."

"But not two months," Janet said. "Even if he rationed it, by now he's run out of food, and Desmond was never much of a hunter. Unless an animal came up and dropped dead at his feet, he'd starve. Then there's the problem of water. How long do you think he would last if he couldn't find any?"

"Not long at all," Fargo had to concede. He turned toward the mountains, a dark purplish mass in the distance. Not even an Apache could endure more than a week without water.

"Yet you're going out after him," Janet said derisively. "And all to spite me. You're almost as silly as he was."

"It will give your daughters some peace of mind." Fargo started to go around her but she placed a hand on his arm, restraining him.

"What's your hurry? It's just you and me. Why not take me for a stroll? Say, down along the river where no one will interrupt us."

Anger simmered in Fargo like boiling water. "You take a lot for granted, Mrs. Hammond."

"Am I to gather you don't find me the least bit attractive?" Janet struck a pose with a hand on her hip and her breasts thrust forward. "I may not be as young as my girls but I can please a man better than they can."

"I'm not interested," Fargo said. He tried to go in but she held on to his sleeve.

"Be careful. There are some insults a woman won't abide and that's one of them. I dare say I could have any man in this pathetic excuse for a town if I put my mind to it."

"Or your body." Fargo pried her fingers off and opened the door. He swore he could feel her eyes boring into him but he did not look back as he walked down the hall. Since he was no longer sleepy he went to the front desk instead of his room.

Fenton Wilson was sorting through a pile of papers, and gave a start. "Fargo! I trust you found the room to your liking?"

"It's fine," Fargo said. He had something else on

his mind. "I need to talk to the marshal. Where can I find his office?"

"Would that there was one," Fenton said. "We don't have a lawman yet. Hell, we don't even have a town council. There's been talk and a few public meetings but nothing has come of it."

"No law at all?" Fargo frowned. Tin badges were scarce west of the Mississippi. For every town or settlement that had one, nine did not.

"What did you want to talk to him about?" Fenton asked.

"The Renegade."

"Is that all? I know as much as anyone. Maybe I can help." Wilson came around the counter and ushered Fargo to a pair of empty chairs near the front window. "Let's see. Where should I start? The first body was found about a month and a half ago. Ted Baker, a prospector, was found by three men out searching for a claim of their own. He had been staked out and carved on and wasn't a pretty sight. Since then, three or four people a week have either been found butchered or gone missing."

"And nothing has been done about it?"

"Are you loco? Everything that can be done, has been done. Search party after search party has gone out, some with dogs, and they always come back empty-handed. A five hundred dollar bounty was posted, then a thousand dollar bounty. Dozens of men have gone out hoping to collect but they come back empty-handed. It's gotten so, people talk about the Renegade as if he's not really human."

"I was told he's an Apache."

"They're not human either, are they?" Fenton said. "But yes, Apache footprints have been found. But the ground is so rocky in the mountains, there's never much sign, and those who have tried to track the Renegade always lose the trail." He paused. "Why all this

38

interest, anyhow? You're not figuring on collecting the bounty yourself, are you?"

"I'm heading out the day after tomorrow to find Desmond Hammond."

"You don't say," Fenton said, and he did not sound particularly pleased. "I credited you with more common sense."

Fargo grinned. "I credited myself with more."

"The Renegade isn't the only Apache you have to watch out for. From time to time war parties have done their share of butchering."

The heat. The dry land. The Renegade. Other Apaches. Janet Hammond. Sam the cook. Fargo was beginning to regret his impulsive decision to stay. "You mentioned trackers. Any I might know?"

"There's Ted Strickland out of Tennessee," Wilson said. "He has a pack of fine hounds but they lost the scent." He paused. "There's Elias Dover from Texas. An old cuss, almost as old as me, but he's scouted for the army and lived with the Cheyenne for a while, I hear tell."

Fargo knew Elias Dover, and yes, he was a damned good tracker. "Where can I find him?"

"Right this moment?" Wilson glanced at the grandfather clock ticking away in a corner. "Most nights he's at the Gila Saloon. Go east four blocks. You can't miss it for the noise."

"Thanks." As Fargo went out, several passersby, two of them women in tight dresses, nearly collided with him. He smiled and doffed his hat, then turned east. A single step was all he took. Then the night exploded in gunfire.

4

Fargo did not know who was shooting or why. His natural reaction, as it was for anyone who had been on the frontier for any length of time, was to drop to his belly and wait for the leaden hail to end. Shootouts were commonplace, and many an innocent bystander took a bullet meant for someone else.

It did not occur to him that *he* might be the target until a slug ripped into the boardwalk to his left and another whizzed over his hat and struck the hotel with a loud *smack*. Two more shots rang out as he rolled and palmed his Colt. By then he had pinpointed where the shots were coming from—the dark mouth of an alley across the street.

He was not the only one who had flattened. Others, less savvy, were frozen in place or gawking about in confusion. A horse reared and whinnied, and it was all its rider could do to stay on.

The instant the firing stopped, Fargo was up and racing for the alley, zigzagging as he ran. He did not see the shooter but that did not stop him from triggering a swift shot into the alley's mouth, a shot rewarded with a yelp of either pain or surprise.

Pedestrians scattered to get out of his way. Riders

reined their animals aside. A man on a sorrel accidentally blundered directly into his path and Fargo had to dig in his heels to avoid colliding with the horse. Then he was past, and the alley was only a few yards away.

Tucking at the waist, Fargo hurtled into the opening. He half hoped to find a body, but there was none. From the rear of the alley came a loud scrape and the patter of running feet. He fired at the sounds.

Another yelp, and Fargo thought he saw a dark shape burst out the far end of the alley. He gave chase but when he reached the other end no one was in sight. He went left, as he thought the figure had done, but although he searched carefully the would-be assassin had slipped away.

Fargo swore to himself. Now he had someone taking potshots at him. He doubted it had been Sam the cook. That left three likely candidates, but begged the question *why*? Were they that mad over the trick he had played on them that they would resort to shooting him? Or was it someone else with a motive he could not begin to suspect?

Reloading, Fargo returned to the main street. Things were back to normal. No one seemed the least little bit excited or upset. People acted as if it were the most perfectly ordinary thing in the world for someone to blast away at any hour of the night or day.

The Gila Saloon was indeed the noisiest in Gila Bend. Tinny piano music blaring from the open windows and a constant hubbub of rowdy voices made it hard for passersby to make themselves heard.

It was by the far the most popular spot in town after the sun went down.

The door was propped open with a broom. Fargo stepped to the right so his back was to the wall and let his eyes adjust to the thick smoke and dim light from half a dozen lanterns.

Lusty drinkers lined the bar. Every table was filled.

Poker, blackjack and faro were the most popular games. Fallen doves mingled freely with the customers, encouraging them to drink more. The two bartenders were busily filling glasses and handing out bottles.

Fargo made for the bar—bartenders were founts of information. If Elias Dover was there, the bartenders were bound to know. He had threaded halfway across the room when a figure at a corner table caught his eye. The man was alone, remarkable in an establishment where every other table was ringed by six or seven people. A mug of beer was in front of him. Beside it was a Sharps rifle, just like the one Fargo used before he switched to the Henry.

He was an older man, and wore buckskins much like Fargo's own. He favored a black hat, not a white one, and a blue bandanna, not red. A salt-and-pepper beard framed a face that had seen everything there was to see and done everything there was to do. A warm smile split his face as he used his left foot to push the chair next to him away from the table.

"As I live and breathe, Skye Fargo! Have a seat, hoss, and tell this old coon what a young buck like you is doin' in this godforsaken hole."

"Pleased to see you again, Elias," Fargo said. "It's been, what, nine months since Fort Laramie?"

"Closer to ten, I reckon," Elias Dover said. He had a gravelly voice. "What's this I hear about you goin' off into the mountains after a peckerwood who couldn't find his own backside without help?"

"Who told you?" Fargo asked.

"Hellfire, hoss, nothin' stays a secret long in these parts. Word that you're here is big news. I was plannin' to look you up tomorrow." The old scout glanced toward the bar. "Barkeep! Bring my friend a whiskey!"

Amazingly, one of the bartenders stopped what he

was doing and brought it right over. "Will there be anything else, Mr. Dover?"

Elias paid him. "Not now, thanks, but keep your ears skinned."

"Yes, sir." The bartender nodded at Fargo and hurried back to help the other one quench the unquenchable thirst of their customers.

"Sir?" Fargo repeated. "What was that all about? And how is it you rate your own table?"

Elias grinned. "You won't believe it, pard, but I've started to take after you. And at my age."

"I've lost your trail."

"You don't like to have it brought up, but you have a reputation as someone better left alone," Elias said. "Well, about a month ago two drunks got too full of themselves and started shootin' up the place. Some locals tried to quiet them down and one was shot for his efforts." Dover treated himself to some beer. "I was buckin' the tiger and content to let the lunkheads alone but then a man sittin' next to me was hit so I got up and bucked both the bastards out in gore. Folks have been walkin' on eggshells around me ever since."

Fargo had been in similar situations more times than he cared to count. "How does it feel to be branded a killer when you're not?"

Dover's mouth quirked. "Now I know what you've been goin' through, hoss, and I'm right sorry I used to tease you about bein' so blamed famous. It's more bother than it's worth."

Another of the old scout's comments had Fargo curious. "You've been here a whole month?"

"Thirty-two days, sixteen hours, and I'd die a happy man if I could remember the minutes," Dover said bleakly.

"Why aren't you off scoutin' for the army?"

Dover's bleak expression worsened. "Then you haven't heard? They've put me out to pasture."

. Fargo didn't believe it. Elias Dover was one of the finest frontiersmen alive and had been working for the army for decades. "You're too ornery to be cut loose," he joked. "Besides, there aren't but five scouts in the whole West who can hold a candle to you."

"And you're one of them," Dover said with sincere respect. "But it's true, hoss. I turned seventy-five this year and the army felt I'm too old to be runnin' around the country fightin' Injuns and such."

"That's plain stupid," Fargo said. Dover was as spry and alert as a man half his age and could go on scouting well into his eighties. "I know at least one scout who is older."

"I know two," Elias Dover said, "but Colonel Patterson wouldn't change his mind no matter how much I cussed or begged."

Fargo had worked with Patterson before. The colonel was military to the marrow, and as dependable an officer as lived. Patterson would never cut Dover lose without a good reason, and Elias's age wasn't one of them. "You didn't really beg him."

"Says the pup young enough to be my grandson," the old scout said. "Hoss, scoutin' is all I know, all I've ever done, all I've ever wanted to do. I figured I had ten more years left in me but the army thought different."

Something didn't quite ring true. If Fargo were in Dover's boots, he would be mad as hell. Or at least bitter at being treated so shabbily. But his friend acted more sad than mad, and not bitter at all. "Want me to look Patterson up after I'm done here and have a talk with him?"

Elias shook his head. "I'm obliged. But it wouldn't do any good. The army has its rules."

Fargo had never heard of one that stipulated a man could not work for the army past a certain age.

"Speakin' of lookin' someone up," Elias changed

the subject, "what can I do for you? Or did you come to the saloon to pat the fannies of some of the doves?"

"The Renegade," Fargo said.

Elias was raising his glass but lowered it again. "Ah. You've heard I went out after him and couldn't bring him to bay?" he glumly asked.

"What can you tell me?"

Elias shrugged. "Nothin' much."

Fargo studied his friend. Tracking a man told a lot about him. How a man walked and did things were clues to his character. "You had to learn something. Is it true the Renegade is an Apache?"

"The prints were made by Apache moccasins, no doubt about that," Elias said, yet an element of uncertainty tinged his voice.

"How far did you track him?"

"About two miles before I lost the sign. A body was found out to Sand Creek. I went there and had a look-see. There's a reward for the Renegade, and I can sure use the money."

Suddenly Fargo thought he understood. Dover wasn't sharing information about the killer because his friend wanted the reward for himself. "Go on."

"The tracks were plain enough the first mile or so," Elias related, "but then he got all tricky to throw pursuers off his scent. Some parts of those mountains are damn near solid rock, and a man doesn't leave any sign at all."

"You only went after him the once?"

Again Elias Dover shrugged. "I was out two weeks. Figure to go out again soon." He paused. "Any chance we could work together?"

The request caught Fargo off guard, and he hesitated.

"We've worked together before," Elias quickly mentioned, "and two sets of eyes are always better than one. If we catch him, I'm more than willin' to share the money. Hell, you can keep most of it for yourself if you want. Just so I have enough to tide me over a spell. I'm not greedy."

Fargo had it, then. His friend was broke, or close to it. Elias had never been the kind to save for a rainy day, and now that he couldn't count on an army paycheck, he was desperate. "You know me better than that. If we go in this together, we split the reward fifty-fifty."

Elias smiled warmly. "You always were the best of us, hoss."

"Fair is fair," Fargo said, realizing he had committed himself whether he wanted to or not.

"Are you headin' out tomorrow?"

"The day after," Fargo said. Primarily because the Ovaro needed the extra day to rest.

"I'll be ready," Elias said. "I've got a good pack animal for whatever grub and whatnot you want to bring."

"Meet me at the stable tomorrow at noon and we'll work everything out," Fargo said. That would give him more than enough time to buy supplies and be at the boarding house by six.

Elias leaned toward him. "I appreciate this, hoss," he said earnestly. "I really and truly do."

"We're friends," Fargo said.

"No, you don't understand—" Elias began, but did not finish what he was about to say. Coughing as if he were embarrassed, he said, "It means a lot to me, is what I'm tryin' to say. More than you can reckon."

They sat and drank and talked about forts they had been to and times they had tracked together and mutual acquaintances. It was close to ten o'clock when Fargo pushed his chair back. "It's been a long day. I'm turning in."

"Maybe you're the one gettin' old." Elias grinned. "I can remember when you would stay up half the night drinkin' and playin' cards and spend twelve hours in the saddle the next day and still be rarin' to go the next night."

"I still can," Fargo said. "I'm not ready to be put out to pasture just yet." He meant it as a jest but a sad look came over Dover.

"We all like to think we will go on forever," Elias said wistfully, "but time has a way of catchin' up with us whether we want it to or not." He shook himself, and smiled. "Don't mind me. I'm gettin' a mite too sentimental in my old age." He spat out the last two words.

Fargo felt sorry for him. He wondered how he would be when he was that old. *If* he lived that long, which was doubtful. More than likely, a bullet or an arrow would end his days long before he had half as many gray hairs as his friend. "The stable at noon," he said, and rose.

After the stuffy air of the smoky saloon, the cool night breeze was invigorating. Fargo stood on the edge of the boardwalk and breathed deep a few times, then turned his boots toward the hotel.

Gila Bend was a beehive of activity. Boomtowns rarely quieted before two or three in the morning.

Wary of another try on his life, Fargo walked close to the buildings and constantly raked the street from end to end. Once he had the feeling eyes were on him and stopped to check every face, every window, every doorway and rooftop. But no one showed the least little interest in him.

Fargo was a block from the Gila Hotel when the angry voice of a drunk drew his gaze to a man and a woman up ahead. The man had backed the woman against a wall and was holding her there while trying to caress her red hair. She struggled to break free but he was much bigger.

Fargo strode toward them.

"—come on, sweetheart," the drunk was saying, his speech thickly slurred. "Give Chester a kiss. Just one and Chester will let you go."

"Please! Take your hands off me!"

"Quit fightin', damn it. What can one kiss hurt? It's not like we don't know each other. I've eaten at the restaurant every day this week." The man ran a hand over her hair and she slapped it away. "I wouldn't do that, were I you. You don't want to make Chester mad. Chester ain't real nice when he's mad."

Fargo drew his Colt. He did not call out. He did not warn the man or politely ask him to let the woman be. "Chester?" he said, and when Chester looked around, he slammed the barrel against the besotted bastard's skull.

Chester oozed to his knees but he was still conscious. "That hurt, you son of a bitch!"

"So will this," Fargo said, and pistol-whipped him again. At the second blow Chester grunted and pitched onto his face, drool dribbling from his mouth and blood trickling from his split scalp.

"I'm in your debt," Maxine Walters said. She was flustered but bravely trying not to show it. Fussing with her dress, she looked down at her tormentor. "I never took him for a lecher."

Fargo twirled the Colt into its holster. "Were you out with him?"

"Goodness, no!" Maxine sounded appalled by the idea. "I was on my way home and he appeared out of nowhere. He wanted to take me for a drink but I refused." She seemed to shiver. "It's gotten so a woman can't walk the streets at night."

"How about if I walk you the rest of the way?" Fargo offered.

"I would like that. I would like that very much." Maxine smiled, then bent and groped about in the shadows. "Where is it? It has to be here somewhere."

"What does?" Fargo asked.

"The gift my admirer gave me. I didn't want it but he made me take it. Ah. Here it is." Maxine straightened with a small velvet-covered box in her hand. She opened it, revealing an ivory pendant in the shape of a rose.

"This admirer of yours must be rich."

"Oh, he does all right for himself," Maxine said absently, then snapped the velvet box shut. "But it's not as if I want him to give me things. I keep telling him not to and he keeps doing it anyway."

The solution to her problem seemed obvious to Fargo. "Give them back."

"I wish I could," Maxine said softly. "But it's not as simple as that. Nothing in life ever is."

"You're an attractive woman," Fargo said. "Men are bound to take an interest."

"If you only knew," Maxine said. "Especially when they find out the woman has been married. They come sniffing around like hungry wolves, hoping she misses it so much, she'll be easy."

Fargo did not ask what "it" was.

"I could just scream sometimes. I tell them no but they pester me anyway. It doesn't help that women are scarce west of the Mississippi."

Fifteen men to every female was the ratio Fargo had read somewhere. "If it bothers you, why not move back East?"

Maxine did not seem to hear. "Scarce or not, it's no excuse for a man to paw a woman when she doesn't want him to. It's no excuse for men thinking a woman is a piece of pie they can take a bite out of any time they care to."

"Not all men are like that," Fargo said, but once again, she did not seem to hear him.

"A saloon girl expects men to take liberties. But women like me shouldn't have to put up with it. All we want is to be left alone to live our lives as we see fit. So what if I was married once? I don't walk around with a sign on my back that says, *'Panting For Love.'*"

Fargo had to laugh. "That would be some sign." He took her elbow and gestured. "Which way to the boardinghouse?"

"Oh. I'm sorry. I'm more rattled than I thought, and when I'm rattled, I talk a lot." Maxine smoothed her hair and led off. "It's at the east end of town, I'm afraid, near the river. It will take a while to get there."

"So? You act as if I wouldn't want your company." To take her mind off the incident with the drunk, Fargo asked, "Where's your son?"

Maxine brightened. "Oh, Donny had to be home by eight. Fenton wants him to work longer hours because Donny is so dependable but I've put my foot down. A boy his age has no business being out and about that late. Who knows what mischief he'll get into?"

"You're a fine mother," Fargo said.

"Am I? Sometimes I wonder. I do the best I can but it's hard for a woman alone. Jobs are hard to come by. Good jobs are even harder to find. I refuse to work at a saloon even though a girl can earn more in one week than I make in a month."

"There are other towns besides Gila Bend," Fargo mentioned. "Places where a woman *can* walk the streets at night, and where she could find a decent job if she looks hard enough."

"I know," Maxine said, "which is why I've been saving every cent I can spare. Another six months, and Donny and I are bound for St. Louis or New Orleans or maybe even New York City."

Her arm was warm against Fargo's. Her shoulder brushed his with every step. The perfume she wore was enough to entice a monk. Add to that the swish of her legs against her dress, and it was only natural Fargo's thoughts started to stray.

"I just want a good life for me and my son," Maxine said longingly. "Is that too much to ask?" She was quiet for a bit. "Lord knows, I don't want to marry again. Not so soon after my husband ran out on me.

But the man who gave me this," she angrily shook the velvet box, "insists I need someone to look after me, as he puts it. As if I'm not able to raise Donny on my own."

Fargo did not know quite what to say. Her personal life was her affair, and he would never suggest how she should live it.

"Women have it hard these days," Maxine lamented. "Either we're supposed to be perfect angels or whores."

"That's not true," Fargo said without thinking.

"Isn't it?" Maxine demanded almost savagely. "What two things do most women become? Either we're expected to be doting wives who are always at our husband's beck and call or we peddle our bodies for money."

Fargo had met women in all lines of work. Seamstresses, waitresses, clerks, bakers, hatmakers, even one who made her living as a stagecoach driver. But he did not bring it up.

"I'm not an angel and I'm not a prostitute," Maxine was saying. "I'm just a woman, with all the needs a woman has." She glanced at him sharply. "What about you? Are you hankering to find yourself a wife and settle down?"

"The only way I would say 'I do' was if I were more booze blind than Chester," Fargo told her.

Maxine smiled for the first time since he rescued her. "At last. An honest man. I was beginning to think there's no such thing." She leaned a little closer. "I'm glad. I like you, and I would hate to think you were no different from every other male."

"I like you too," Fargo said for want of anything else. "But I should warn you. I'm no angel, either. Far from it."

"I was hoping you would say that," Maxine said, and without any hint of what she had in mind, she rose on her toes and pecked him on the cheek.

"Were you now?" Fargo grinned. Women could be mad as riled rattlesnakes one second, as sweet as brown sugar the next. Even more bewildering, they had the uncanny ability to think in fifty different directions at once. Small wonder they baffled men so much.

Soon the busiest part of town was behind them. They turned right at the next junction and left at the one after that and followed a narrow rutted road that wound along the river until they came to a sprawling frame house that sat off by itself under spreading maple trees.

"There's the boardinghouse," Maxine said. "Donny and I have rooms at the back." She slowed, and cleared her throat. "I don't suppose you would like to come in?"

Fargo admired her lustrous hair, the sweep of her full bosom, and the swell of her thighs. "I'd like nothing better."

5

The rooms were more nicely furnished than was customary for a boardinghouse. Curtains decorated the window, two fine lamps glowed brightly, and there was even carpet on the floors.

Only two rooms, though, Fargo noticed, which puzzled him. Maybe Maxine's invitation was not the kind of invite he took it to be.

The main room was a combination parlor and kitchen. To one side stood a small stove that also served to heat the rooms in the winter. A settee was the centerpiece, and curled up on it, sound asleep, was young Donny Walters.

Maxine smiled at the sight of him. Going over, she bent and stroked his hair and said softly, "Donny? Donny? Wake up, dear."

The boy stirred and mumbled but did not open his eyes.

"Donny," Maxine said, louder, and gave his shoulder a shake. That did it. He sat upright and blinked and scratched his head.

"Ma! What time is it? Is it morning already?" Then Donny saw Fargo and he gave a start. "Mr. Fargo? What's he doing here?"

"He walked me home and I've offered him a cup of tea," Maxine said. "It's why I woke you up. I'll sleep here tonight. You take the bed."

"Are you sure?" Donny said, trying to stifle a yawn and failing. "You always say the bed is more comfortable."

Maxine kissed him on the forehead. "I'm sure. Now scoot in there and I'll tuck you in."

"Whatever you want." Donny slowly rose. He was not fully awake and his legs were unsteady. Then he saw the velvet-covered box. "What's that Ma?"

"Nothing," Maxine said.

"It's from him, isn't it? He gave you another gift?"

"Go to bed, Donny."

"Why won't he leave you alone? Why does he keep at you when you've told him over and over you don't want him?"

"We shouldn't discuss personal matters when we have a guest," Maxine said.

"It's not right, I tell you," Donny persisted. "I have half a mind to talk to him about it tomorrow."

"You'll do no such thing," Maxine said sternly. "It's my problem. I will deal with it."

"Your problems are my problems," Donny said. "Besides, I don't like how he looks at you. Other men do that and you get mad. Him, you don't say a word."

"Life is complicated somctimes, son," Maxine said. "We do things we don't want to do because we have to."

"Not me," Donny said. "When I don't want to do something, I darned well don't do it."

"Oh?" Maxine smiled. "What about the dishes? Who keeps giving me a hard time about having to dry them and put them away?"

"That's different," Donny said sullenly, but he stopped arguing and shuffled toward the doorway at the other end of the room. "I can't help it I care about you."

Now it was Maxine who gave a start. She caught up

to him and embraced him from behind. "I appreciate that. I honestly and truly do. And I'm sorry I won't let you give him a piece of your mind. But this is an adult matter, son."

"So you keep saying," Donny grumbled. "But if you ask me, most adults aren't any more mature than me."

They went into the bedroom, and Fargo parted the curtains and looked out. The window faced north, and a grove of trees. He was about to let the curtains close when something moved off in the darkness. He tensed, thinking someone had followed them from town but the next moment two deer stepped into the starlight. "Someone shoots at you and you're jumping at shadows," he said to himself.

"What was that?"

Fargo turned. Maxine had come back in. "Your boy has a point. There are a lot of jackasses running around."

"Don't I know it." Maxine took off her shawl and hung it on a peg. "How about that tea I mentioned?"

Of all the drinks in creation, Fargo liked tea the least. Maybe it was because his mother had made it for him so often when he was young that he grew tired of it. Or maybe it was that tea could not hold a candle to what he would rather have. "Any chance of having coffee instead?"

"I believe I have some, yes," Maxine said, going to a cupboard near the stove. "I don't drink it much, myself, since it tends to keep me up nights and I need all the sleep I can get."

"I don't suppose you'll tell me?" Fargo said.

"Tell you what?" Maxine glanced over her shoulder, then at the bedroom. "Oh. No. Like I told Donny, it's personal. I've handled it so far and I'll go on handling it until I have enough money saved for us to move."

"The man shouldn't force himself on you," Fargo tried again.

"You're sweet. Do you know that?" Maxine took the coffee from the cupboard and placed it on a small table. "But it's different for women than it is for men. We can't punch someone in the nose for being obnoxious. We have to be subtle."

"Suit yourself," Fargo said, "but the offer holds for as long as I'm in Gila Bend. There's nothing like kicking a man's teeth in to get his attention."

"I mentioned punching his nose," Maxine said, then glanced at him again, her eyes narrowed. "You don't put up with much, do you?"

"No." Fargo let it go at that.

"I wish I had the same luxury," Maxine said. "But I couldn't pistol-whip someone or kick their teeth in even if I wanted to. I'm not made that way."

"I can leave if you want."

Maxine spun so quickly, she nearly spilled the grounds she was transferring to the coffeepot. "Oh, my, no! I didn't mean anything by that. Please. Stay."

Fargo went to the settee and sat. It was hard and rough and would not be comfortable to sleep on.

"You misunderstood," Maxine had gone on. "I'm not a violent person, is all. Oh, I get mad just like everyone else, but I can never bring myself to lift a hand against another human being. Even when they deserve it."

"It's a good thing you haven't run into the Renegade," Fargo made light of her somber attitude.

"Believe me, I know it. If Apaches had jumped us on the way here, I'd have been a lamb for the slaughter." Max placed the pot on the stove. "Sometimes I think there is such a thing as being *too* nice."

"Nice has nothing to do with it," Fargo said. "It's about survival. I don't go around killing people for the hell of it and I get mighty upset when someone tries to kill me."

Maxine checked that the stove had wood in it. "But

my suitor isn't trying to kill me. He only wants me to marry him."

"He's still making your life miserable." Fargo removed his hat and hung it from a corner of the settee. "I won't be put on, ever. And it riles me to see others put on. Something in my nature, I guess."

"You should be a lawman." Maxine stepped to the settee and sat an arm's length from him. "Isn't that what they do? Protect others from being imposed on?"

"They uphold the law," Fargo said. "There's a difference." The biggest being that a marshal or a sheriff could act only after a law had been broken. By then it was often too late to help the victim.

"You're an intriguing man," Max complimented him. "I don't think I've ever met anyone quite like you."

Fargo was uncomfortable with her making more of it than she should. "There are a lot like me."

Maxine smoothed her dress where it draped over her knees and sat back with her hands in her lap. She glanced at him out of the corner of her eyes, then closed her eyes and grimaced as if she were in pain. Then she opened them again and smiled. "I'm sorry. Please don't hold it against me."

"Hold what?" Fargo said, puzzled by her behavior.

"My nerves. I haven't had a man over since my husband ran out on me. A lot have wanted to come over but I wouldn't let them."

"I'm honored." Fargo was rewarded with a blush. Reaching over, he placed his hand on hers. "But I don't bite. And I don't force myself on a woman. She has to want to be with me."

"I do," Maxine said. "Very much so. It's just that I haven't, well—" She stopped and blushed even darker. "Look at me. I'm acting like a girl on her first date. You would think I had never been kissed."

"You brought me here to kiss you?" Fargo said, pretending to be shocked.

Maxine burst into laughter that went on and on, much longer than Fargo's remark called for, until finally she stopped and dabbed at her eyes with a sleeve, saying, "Thank you for putting me at ease."

"You're easy to talk to," Fargo said, and meant it. Not that talking was uppermost on his mind.

"Thank you!" Maxine said. "I'm out of practice. It's been so long. I just, well." She did not go on. Suddenly standing, she said, "I'll check on the coffee."

Fargo inwardly smiled. She had put the pot on only a minute ago. Rising, he stepped up behind her and looped his right arm around her waist. She stiffened and gasped, but then, when all he did was stand there, their bodies barely touching, she relaxed and looked over her shoulder with twin twinkles in her eyes.

"Next time warn me. I about fainted."

"You're fretting for no reason," Fargo said.

"How is that?" Maxine inquired.

Fargo nodded his head toward the bedroom. "Do you honestly think we can with him so close? Would you even want to?" Most mothers wouldn't run the risk.

An impish grin curled her luscious lips. "Now who is fretting? I have it all worked out. You'll see."

They stood there, quietly. Between the stove and her body, Fargo grew almost uncomfortably warm.

"Is it me or should I maybe crack the window?" Maxine abruptly asked.

"Be my guest." Fargo reluctantly released her and leaned against the table with his arms folded across his chest. He liked how her hips swayed, and how her bosom jiggled as she raised the window a couple of inches.

"It's a beautiful night," Maxine commented while peering out. "We should go for a stroll after a while."

"Ah," Fargo said, and grinned.

Maxine came back but she did not go to the stove. She came straight toward him and when she was close enough she placed her hands on his shoulders and rose onto her toes to kiss him full on the lips. A fleeting kiss, to be sure, offering a tantalizing hint of soft lips and the pleasure they would later incite.

"Sorry," Maxine said. "I couldn't resist."

"That makes two of us." Pulling her close, Fargo fused his mouth to hers. He flicked his tongue across her lips and they parted. Her tongue met his in silken swirls that ended a minute later with Maxine breathing heavily with her forehead against his arm, and he with a stirring in his groin.

"That was nice," Maxine said softly. "Has anyone ever told you that you are a marvelous kisser?"

Fargo caressed her red hair and she gave a little shudder.

"You must have a lot of experience."

"Not that much," Fargo said with a straight face. He hadn't played poker all those years for nothing.

"I don't have much, either, I'm afraid. There was my husband, and before him a boy I courted but we never really did much."

"Stop apologizing for yourself," Fargo said. "You're fine as you are. If I wanted a woman with a lot of experience I'd be with a dove from the saloon."

"Have you ever been with a dove before?" Maxine asked.

Fargo sensed she was fishing for information no man should divulge. "One or two," he said. Which was true as far as it went. All he left out was the "hundred."

"My husband used to sneak off to the saloon every chance he got. I didn't find out until the very end. It crushed me, I admit. I had never refused him once in all the years we were married. And maybe I'm not the most experienced woman on earth, but I did my best to please him. Yet it wasn't enough."

"Forget about him," Fargo advised. "You're making a new life for yourself."

"I try. But he was a big part of my life for so long. I had Donny by him. I loved him once, or I wouldn't have married him. But my love meant nothing to him." She paused. "Looking back, I think the only reason he ever married me was because it was the only way he could get me into bed."

Fargo had heard enough about the husband for one night. Gently clasping her chin, he tilted her face up to his and kissed her again, this time kneading her bottom as their tongues entwined.

Maxine cooed deep in her throat, and when they parted for air, she was flushed, her cheeks positively rosy. "Oh my," she breathed. "The things you do to me."

Fargo could say the same. He had a bulge in his pants that promised to grow a lot bigger.

Then, out of the blue, Maxine said, "Oh! I almost forgot. I wanted to ask if you know a man by the name of Amos Spack?"

"I've met him," Fargo said, wondering what Spack had to do with anything.

"I was going to tell you about it tomorrow when I saw you," Maxine explained. "Spack and those two shadows of his, Toad and Grub, were at the restaurant tonight. Early, about five or so. They come in a lot, those three. I don't like them much, but they've never once made a lewd remark or put their hands on me, like some do."

"Why did you ask me about him?"

"Because they were talking about you. I was walking past their table and overheard Spack mention your name. I thought maybe I was mistaken, so I walked by them again, and one of the big ones, Toad, was saying something about you and how they had made a mistake."

"What else?"

"That's all, I'm afraid. Spack noticed I was listening and hushed the other two up, and I went on about my work. As they were leaving, Spack gave me a dirty look but he didn't say anything." Maxine smiled. "I thought you would like to know. Any idea what it was about?"

"No," Fargo confessed. "What can you tell me about those three? How long have they been in Gila Bend?"

"They were here before I arrived," Maxine said. "I have no idea what they do for a living although I seem to recall hearing somewhere that they gamble a lot. I've never once seen any of them with a woman so I guess they limit their vices."

"Do they spend most of their time in town or are they away a lot?"

Maxine's forehead knit. "I don't keep track of what they do. But I have noticed that they'll be at the restaurant every day for a week or so, then won't show up again for two whole weeks. Why?"

"I just wondered," Fargo said, and wondered about something else. "Have there been any killings besides those blamed on the Renegade?"

"Gila Bend has had its share of shooting affrays," Maxine said. "But if you mean prospectors being murdered, yes, I think there were a few before the Renegade started butchering people."

"Is there a town newspaper?" Fargo asked. That would be the place to go to find out more.

"I'm afraid not. There was talk of a man coming here to start one but he changed his mind and went to California instead. Something to do with him being allergic to Apaches."

The coffeepot was hissing and spitting. Maxine turned to the stove and then to the cupboard and took down a pair of cups and saucers. She opened a drawer and selected two spoons. Then she placed a sugar bowl on the table. "If you don't mind my asking, how much longer will you be in Gila Bend?"

"It depends on how long it takes to track down the Renegade."

"The Renegade?" Maxine looked up. "But the word around town is that the Hammond siblings hired you to find their missing father."

"That, too," Fargo said.

"How can you stand there so calmly? Aren't you the least bit worried? The Renegade is a killer."

"He has to be stopped or a lot more will die."

"But why must *you* be the one? What are all those prospectors to you that you should even care? Why risk your life for people you haven't even met?" Maxine studied him anew. "What kind of man are you, anyhow?"

"There you go again," Fargo said, and sighed. "I'm a scout. Tracking is what I do. No, I've never met any of the prospectors, but I can't ignore what the Renegade has done. The Hammonds believe he killed their father."

"You're taking your life in your hands."

"I'll have help. Elias Dover is going with me. Maybe you've heard of him."

"The old man who used to work for the army," Maxine said. "Sure. He's been in the restaurant a few times." Almost as an afterthought she added, "It's a shame he never learned to read."

"What are you talking about?" Fargo distinctly recalled the time, it must have been five years ago, when Elias got a letter from a sister back in the States and read part of it aloud one night as they sat around their campfire.

"Didn't you know? Mr. Dover can't read a lick. He told me so himself the first time he came in. I gave him a menu and he handed it back and asked me to read it to him. Said he never went to school."

The implication stunned Fargo. "He wasn't joshing you?"

"Why would he josh about a thing like that? If anything, he was embarrassed, and kept saying how sorry he was to put me to the trouble." Maxine watched bubbles perking in the top of the pot. "Are you about ready for your coffee?"

"Didn't you say something about a stroll?" Fargo said. "Maybe we should get that out of the way first."

Maxine looked at him. She wrung her hands a moment, then lowered them and said, "Why not? I know just the spot. Let me check on Donny first." She hurried into the bedroom.

Fargo went to the door and opened it. A cool breeze fanned his face and stirred the whangs on his buckskins. To his right, off through some trees, the river was visible, a shimmering ribbon as dark as blood. To his left was the stand where he had seen the does, but they were gone.

"Skye?" Maxine emerged, wrapping her shawl about her. "He's sound asleep, the poor dear. Wilson works his boys hard." She quietly closed the door, then offered her arm.

Fargo took it and she guided their steps toward the river, walking slowly, her face tilted back with her eyes half closed.

"It's so peaceful here at night." The starlight played over her lovely features, accenting her cheeks and the fullness of her lips. "I often come down to the river just to sit and think after I've tucked my son in."

"Is that wise in Apache country?" Fargo brought up.

"They never venture this close to town."

"You hope." It had been Fargo's experience that Apaches could sneak up close enough to touch most whites without the whites being aware of it. Apaches were masters at stealth.

"Let's not talk about hostiles," Maxine said. "Let's

not talk about my admirer or my husband or the Renegade or any of that." She leaned over and rested her head on his shoulder. "I want to forget the ugliness for a while. I want to forget all the horror in the world."

Easier said than done, Fargo thought to himself. The horror was always there, always ready to pounce on those who let down their guard.

"I want this to be perfect," Maxine said. "Something I'll always remember. Always cherish."

"It's a good thing you like how I kiss," Fargo said.

Maxine laughed softly, then kissed him on the cheek. "How a man like you never married, I will never know."

"There are a lot of reasons," Fargo was honest with her. "I like to wander. I'm never in one place that long. I like women. Lots of women. I don't know as I could limit myself to one."

Maxine raised her eyes to his. "You've never been in love, then? Not once in your entire life? How sad."

"There was one time—" Fargo said, and stopped.

"I see. And it didn't work out? That's too bad. We all deserve one chance at true happiness. But who am I to talk? I thought I had true happiness and it turned out to be a sham."

"I thought we weren't going to talk about your marriage," Fargo reminded her. They were following a trail between tall cottonwoods. This close to the river, insects and a few frogs broke the stillness.

"I'm always scared I'll stumble on a snake," Maxine mentioned. "Is it true rattlesnakes do most of their hunting at night?"

Fargo nodded. "So do mountain lions and other meat eaters. Something to keep in mind when you take your little walks."

The trees ended at a grassy bank. Below flowed the Gila River, gurgling and whispering as if it were alive. The stars overhead were bright and clear, the lights of the town to the west.

"It is so pretty here," Maxine said. "So peaceful." Rather shyly she mentioned, "I've never brought anyone else here except Donny."

Fargo turned her so she faced him. "If you're having second thoughts, now is the time to back out."

Maxine's arms rose around his neck and she kissed him with a fierce intensity born of long-denied passion. When she stepped back, she asked huskily, "Are you just going to stand there or must I do it all myself?"

6

For a few moments Fargo stared at her, at the sheen of starlight in her lustrous hair, at her flushed up-turned features, ripe with desire, at the enticing curve to her bosom and the promise of her thighs. She was like a peach waiting to be bit into, and he was famished.

Enfolding Maxine in his arms, Fargo molded his mouth to hers in a kiss that never seemed to end. Her lips were deliciously soft, her tongue explored every inch of his mouth. Her fingers sculpted his shoulders, then traced delicate paths up his neck to his hair. Without breaking their kiss she removed his hat and dropped it to the grass.

The heat her body gave off was incredible. Her breasts were pressed against his chest, and he swore he could feel her nipples harden through his shirt. When he cupped a mound and tweaked a jutting tack, she cooed softly deep in her throat and wriggled her hips.

Fargo's hunger climbed. He was not a monk. To him, indulging in carnal pleasure, as someone called it, was as much a part of life as breathing. Were he to live to be one hundred he would never get enough.

Once, on a Kansas City street corner, Fargo heard

a man of the cloth go on and on about how cravings of the flesh were evil. The only real purpose, the man claimed, was to make babies. The rest of the time people were supposed to deny they had bodies, which struck Fargo as peculiar. If that was all there was to it, why had the Almighty made women so breathtakingly beautiful?

He thought of that now as he lowered his other hand to the junction of Maxine's legs and began to stroke her thighs. She was warmer there than anywhere, and growing warmer by the second.

Fargo never had been one to apologize for his needs. When he was thirsty, he drank. When his stomach growled, he ate. When his manhood hardened and he got that familiar constriction in his throat, he gave rein to his need.

Maxine's hunger matched his. Her fingers were everywhere, caressing, probing, uncovering. She undid his gun belt and lowered it beside his hat, then hitched at his shirt and slid her hands up under it. She liked to rub her palms over his washboard abdomen; she did it for minutes on end. She also had a playful streak. When he pinched one of her nipples, she pinched one of his.

Her lips strayed to his neck and latched there. She swirled her tongue around and around, sending tiny shivers shooting through him. Her breath was hot enough to melt wax.

Fargo's left hand drifted around her thigh to her backside. He cupped each of her buns in turn, kneading them as a baker kneaded bread dough. Maxine moaned and ground herself into him.

"I want you so much."

The feeling was mutual. Fargo began undoing her buttons and stays. She wore a dress with tiny buttons at the front and more tiny buttons at the back, to the point where it took iron self-control not to seize the material in both hands and rip it from her body.

And what a body! When at length Fargo peeled away her undergarments like the skin of a banana, out burst two perfectly round globes, breasts so exquisitely formed, with nipples that arced upward, he could not resist inhaling one and lathering it as if it were candy. He lathered and kissed and kissed and lathered until both her mounds heaved with unbridled release and she shivered at his slightest touch.

Fargo debated whether to take her dress all the way off and decided against it. They were far enough from town that it should be safe but there was always the chance, however slim, that someone might wander by and she would need to cover herself as quickly as possible. Instead, he hiked at her dress and parted her chemise and drawers, and was there.

At the contact of Fargo's fingers with her slit, Maxine gasped and arched her back into a bow. For a few seconds she held perfectly still; then she melted against him and clung to his broad shoulders, overcome by rapture.

Fargo slid his finger along her slit to her tiny knob. He only had to flick it once to provoke her into quaking paroxysms of release. Mewing sounds escaped her throat and her nails bit into his flesh.

Lightly running his fingertip back and forth, Fargo let her anticipation, and his own, climb. Meanwhile her lips had glued themselves to his ear and she was giving it the same attention he gave her breasts.

Fargo lost himself in her charms. In her yielding mouth and her smooth skin, in her perfect breasts and the wondrous smoothness of her thighs. By then she was drenched and her bottom could not stay still if her life depended on it.

"Take me, please," Maxine husked.

Fargo carefully lowered her to the grass. As soft as any down mattress, it was cool to the touch. Lying on his side, Fargo kissed her nipples and her flat belly and dipped his tongue into her navel. She gripped

68

his hair with such force, she nearly ripped it out by the roots.

"You are magnificent!"

Fargo was only beginning. He lavished kisses from her waist to her neck and back down again. He rubbed a cheek against her crinkly hairs, then nuzzled her thighs. They parted to admit him but he was not quite ready yet. Instead, he inserted a finger into her smoldering core.

"Ah! Yes!" Maxine whispered, her eyelids fluttering. "Like that!"

Fargo inserted a second finger and held them still but only for a few teasing seconds. Then he plunged both in to the knuckle and drew them out again, or almost. Maxine's response was to lever her body up off the ground and softly cry out.

Old instincts were hard to break. Fargo raised his head and looked around. They were still alone, still had the bank and the river and the stars to themselves. He must stop worrying so much, he told himself. But he had already been shot at once that night and did not care to be a target again.

Maxine tugged at his pants. She wanted them down and she wanted them down now. When they did not slide fast enough to suit her, she plunged a hand in and grasped what she was after.

It was Fargo's turn to gasp and shiver as she moved her hand in ways that drove men to the brink of release. When she cupped him even lower, he thought it was over. But somehow he snipped his inner fuse so he could last a while yet. Fastening his mouth to a nipple, he pumped his fingers ever faster and ever harder and was soon rewarded with a tremulous whine and her second release of the night. This one was more violent than the first. She clung to him while her body shook from head to painted toenails and her thighs clamped on his hand like a satin vise.

Fargo stopped stroking only when Maxine subsided

and lay quietly panting in small breaths. He could not help thinking that any man who would leave a woman like this was dumb as a stump.

Her fingers stirred. They renewed their acquaintance with his pole, running lightly up and down it. The constriction in his throat returned, more pronounced than before. He helped her slide his pants down to his knees. Rather than take them off, he simply knelt where he was, arranging himself between her legs.

"Now?" Maxine requested.

"Now," Fargo said, and rubbed his member along her slit. Her ankles locked behind his back and she scooted her bottom closer so it was that much easier for him to do what he did next—to penetrate her, bit by bit, until his sword was fully sheathed in her scabbard.

"Yesssssssss!" Maxine exclaimed. "At last! At long last!"

Fargo glanced toward the boardinghouse, then gripped her hips and commenced rocking in a rhythm as old as humankind. He went slowly at first, savoring each stroke, stoking their mutual inner fires by gradually rising degrees.

Maxine closed her eyes and shuddered. Her nails dug deeper than ever, and on top of that, she suddenly bit him on the shoulder hard enough to draw blood.

Firming his holds, Fargo rammed into her as if he were seeking to cleave her in half.

"Ohhhhh!" Maxine moaned, rising to meet each of his thrusts with marching ardor. "Fill me!"

The world around them blurred. This was the moment Fargo liked best, or second best, and the time when they were most vulnerable. Anyone lurking in the woods could easily pick them off. But he would not stop, he *could* not stop, even if a small part of him wanted to, and no part of him did.

This was the nectar that sweetened everyday life. This was the antidote to the monotony of day in, day out routine. *This* was better than whiskey and better than poker, and he could never be one of those who went their whole life without because they believed it was somehow evil or vile.

It was pleasure, through and through.

Maxine reached the summit for the third time. Another soft cry signaled her release, and she grasped him as a woman who was drowning would grasp a log that was her only hope of staying afloat. She groaned, then sobbed, and when she was done, she collapsed, spent and exhausted.

Fargo still had to reach the brink. He continued to stroke, continued to ram into her. The slap-slap-slap of their bodies became a steady cadence. Maxine looked up at him in wonder, her lovely eyes widening. Then she trembled and mouthed inarticulate cries of ecstasy. He moved faster and faster and felt her lips on his neck. Something as simple as that, yet it triggered his climax. There was no holding back if he wanted to. He was a redwood and Niagara Falls rolled into one. Every nerve tingled. Every fiber of his being was as alive as alive could be.

Afterward, they lay side by side, the breeze cool on their sweaty bodies. Fargo forced himself to sit up, pull his pants on, and strap on the Colt. Then he sank back down and let his thoughts drift where they would.

"Thank you," Maxine whispered.

"Any time," Fargo said.

"I might well take you up on that tomorrow," Maxine teased, but she was in earnest. "We are still going out, aren't we?"

"Unless a buckboard runs over me." Fargo had shut his eyes and was close to dozing off. He felt marvelously fine, as he always did, after.

"I wish you weren't going to try and find Desmond Hammond," Maxine unexpectedly mentioned. "I'll worry about you the whole time you're gone."

"No strings, remember?"

"I didn't mean it like that," Maxine quickly said, yet it was plain to Fargo that was exactly how she did mean it. She snuggled against him. "Mmmm. You smell nice. I like your sweat."

Fargo thought that silly but he did not say so. Her chatter was keeping him from falling asleep but maybe that was just as well. There they were, out in the open on a riverbank in the dead of night in the middle of Apache country. He could think of stupider things but it would take some doing.

Maxine was one of those ladies who could not stop talking after she had shared herself. "That was the best ever. I mean it. My husband was all right but he lost interest in me years ago and never liked it much after that."

The last thing Fargo cared to hear about was her relations with the idiot. "There's more than one stallion in the pasture."

"Yes. I see your point. But women don't have the same choices men do. If we cozy up to more than one we're only fit for saloon work, or worse."

"It won't always be that way," Fargo said, thinking of the move she had planned, but evidently she thought he meant something else.

"I pray to God you're right. I pray that one day women have the right to do as they please without being branded harlots. When we can vote, that's when it will change. For too long we have been denied the same rights as you men. That's wrong, and terribly unfair."

Was she talking politics? Fargo sleepily wondered. Maybe he should pinch himself to see if he was dreaming.

"I should get back. I don't like leaving Donny alone

too long. He gets scared at night by himself. He pretends he's not but I know better."

Fargo heard rustling and cracked his eyelids. She was pulling herself together and smoothing her chemise.

"Besides which, I wouldn't put it past my husband to try and take Donny away from me. He wanted to but I wouldn't let him. I told him no son of mine was going to go live with a hussy like her." Maxine paused. "I'm sorry. I'm babbling, aren't I? I don't mean to. I'm just so happy."

Fargo sighed and sat back up. No one had to beat him with a sledge. He began tucking his shirt in.

"Did you ever want to be anything other than a scout?"

"You ask that now?" Fargo said, and shrugged. "I never gave it much thought. I like what I do. I like the mountains, the prairie, the desert. I like seeing new country." He could never be a store clerk or a bank teller, never chain himself to a counter or a desk all day long.

"I envy you," Maxine said. "You're as free as the wind. You can go anywhere your whims take you. Most of us aren't so lucky."

Luck had nothing to do with it, Fargo reflected. He just went out and did it. Those who made a scapegoat of luck tended to use it as a crutch to justify not doing what they should do to make their dreams come true.

"I can't wait to leave Gila Bend," Maxine said. "As soon as I have enough, we're off to a new life in a new city. Donny will go to school and make something of himself. I might find a new man." She stopped. "Oh. Sorry. I guess I shouldn't have said that."

"Why not?" Fargo responded. "You're too young and too pretty to spend the rest of your life alone."

"You could always look us up if you wanted," Maxine said.

Fargo did not reply. She was fishing and he refused

to nibble at the bait. He jammed his hat back on his head and pulled the rim low over his eyes. "Are you about ready?"

"Almost." Maxine sounded disappointed. "I have more buttons than you do."

"Bigger tits, too."

There were several seconds of shocked silence, then Maxine laughed heartily and put a hand on his arm. "You are a card, Skye Fargo. There was a time when I would have slapped you for being so crude."

"I'd have slapped you back." Fargo rose and adjusted his gun belt. In the river something splashed, a fish or a frog, perhaps. From the north wafted the yip of a lonesome coyote.

Maxine was a long time doing herself up. She had to button every button, had to have every stay in place, and her hair had to be just so. In case, as she told him, "Donny isn't asleep. I don't want him thinking his mother was fooling around."

They walked back shoulder to shoulder, Maxine's hand in his. "I will never forget this night as long as I live."

Fargo was thinking about tomorrow and the preparations he must make before heading out with Elias Dover. The faint crack of a twig brought his head up. It came from the trees north of the boardinghouse. The deer, he reckoned. Then a shadow detached itself from a trunk and he threw an arm around Maxine and practically hurled her to the ground while diving flat himself.

The night rocked to the blast of gunfire. Two, three, four shots, one after the other, a rifle fired as rapidly as the would-be killer could shoot.

Lead buzzed over them. Fargo returned fire and saw the shadow whirl and bolt. "Stay down!" he told Maxine. Heaving up into a crouch, he gave chase. This made twice someone had tried to blow windows in his skull. He would be damned if there would be a third time.

A darkling silhouette briefly appeared but Fargo didn't shoot. He wanted to be sure. Sprinting flat out, he swerved to avoid a waist-high bush and nearly collided with a log. Vaulting over it, he landed lightly on the balls of his feet and ran on. Up ahead, the undergrowth crackled.

Fargo had a fair hunch who it was. He had made only one enemy since arriving in Gila Bend. Two, if he counted the drunk he had pistol-whipped. But it had to be Amos Spack. The ferret-faced killer had been mad as hell at being outfoxed. Mad enough to want to silence him.

A pine loomed in Fargo's path and he skirted it in two bounds. Suddenly a flash flared to the northwest and another slug missed Fargo's ear by inches. This time when he fired back he thought he heard a grunt.

The figure spun and sped off. Fargo could not see it clearly but he was close enough to shed doubts on his hunch. Whoever it was, the shooter was much taller and broader than Spack. It had to be someone else. Two possibilities came to mind, and Fargo yearned for a clear shot to find out.

The bushwhacker was heading west toward town. Fargo sought to narrow the gap but his long-legged enemy held his own.

If anyone had heard the shots, they ignored them. At that time of night, those already indoors had no inclination to poke their heads out and have it take a stray bullet. And those still up had other things on their minds.

The figure barreled into a dense tract of woodland. Gruff laughter fell on Fargo's ears, and then the thud of hooves.

"Damn!" Fargo swore, and fairly flew. He glimpsed the horse and rider but there was too much intervening brush for him to fire. He swore again, more luridly, and slanted to the left hoping for the clear shot he needed but there were too many low tree limbs. Thwarted, he came to a stop and stood with his hands on his knees, catching his breath, as more mocking mirth came out of the dark.

"This one is yours," Fargo said aloud. But there would be another, and the next time it would end in his favor.

Maxine was nowhere in sight when Fargo reached the boardinghouse but she must have been watching for him out the window because the door jerked open as he was about to knock.

"Are you all right?"

Before Fargo could answer she had her arms around him and her lips pressed to his neck.

"I was so worried! Who was it? Why did they try to kill us?"

"They were after me, not you," Fargo said. "Whoever it was will try again. So it might be best if we don't see each other until I've settled things."

Drawing back, Max studied him. "That's sweet of you. But I refuse to be scared off. If I want to spend time with you, I will."

"What about your son?"

"What about him?" Maxine rejoined, and blinked. "Oh. They might try when he's with us, is that what you're saying?" She gazed bitterly into the woods. "I wouldn't want that. And I wouldn't want him made an orphan, either."

"I can still treat the both of you to a meal at the restaurant," Fargo offered. They should be safe enough there.

"You wouldn't mind if I brought Donny?" Maxine was pleased and it showed.

"Six o'clock," Fargo said, and touched his hat brim. He turned to go but she bestowed a last lingering kiss. Troubled she was becoming too attached to him, he headed back. If she was, it wasn't his fault. He had made his sentiments as plain as he could.

Fargo walked with his hand on his Colt. At any instant another gunshot might ring out. But his precaution proved unwarranted. Presently, he was making his way down the main street, close to the boardwalk but not on it so he had an unobstructed view of all the doorways and windows. He would not make it easy for them.

A lot of people were still about. Many had indulged in hard liquor, and some were walking around with whiskey bottles in hand. No one showed any interest in him. He reached the hotel without incident. One of Fenton Wilson's boys was on duty at the front desk. The boy nodded as Fargo strode by.

"Hold up, there!" From out of a recessed door beyond the counter came Wilson, no trace of fatigue about him.

"Don't you ever sleep?" Fargo asked.

"I could say the same about you," Fenton said, smiling. "Where have you been off to? Drinking?"

Normally Fargo kept his personal doings to himself but in this instance he didn't mind saying, "I spent some time with Maxine."

"You don't say," Fenton said. "She is a prize, that one. Her boy is well behaved for someone his age. And smart as a whip, too. I never have to tell him anything twice."

Fargo was tired and anxious to turn in. "See you in the morning," he said, and started for the stairs.

"Wait," Fenton said. "I thought you should know three men were here earlier asking about you."

Fargo's fatigue evaporated. "Did they say who they were?"

"They didn't have to. I've seen them around town plenty of times. It was Amos Spack and his two shadows, Toad and Charlie Grub."

"Grub is his real name?" Fargo had assumed it was a nickname.

"Bad characters, all three," Fenton said. "No one halfway decent will have anything to do with them. Spack has a temper worse than a rattler's and the other two are fond of beating on people with their fists. Not long ago they were in a saloon brawl and Toad got some man in a bear hug and fractured half his ribs." He cocked his head. "If you don't mind my big nose, why would vermin like that be asking about you?"

"What did they want to know?"

"Your room number and whether you were in or not," Fenton said. "I wouldn't tell them. Spack puffed up like a bull snake and called me all sorts of names but I still wouldn't so he left in a huff."

"How long ago was this?" Fargo asked.

"An hour and a half, maybe less," Wilson said. "Grub hung around out front for a while; then he disappeared." The hotel owner smirked. "Strange friends you have."

"They're no friends of mine." Fargo took the stairs two at a stride. Preoccupied with thoughts of Amos Spack, he fished in a pocket for the key and inserted it into the lock. He was opening the door when a noise from within caused him to tense and palm the Colt. Quickly stepping to one side, he pushed on the door with a toe.

Someone was there, all right.

Janet Hammond had laid claim to his bed, the quilt around her waist, naked from the waist up. Smiling sweetly, she greeted him with, "It's about time you got back, handsome. I was ready to start without you."

7

Ordinarily the sight of a bare-breasted woman stirred Fargo where it would stir most any man. But he did not particularly like Janet Hammond, and he was in no mood for any of her shenanigans. "What the hell do you think you're doing?"

Janet grinned coyly. "I could say I climbed into the wrong bed by mistake. Would that satisfy you?"

Fargo stood in the doorway making no move to enter or to close the door.

"What's the matter?" Janet asked. "Most men would be delighted. I might be pushing forty but I'm a fine figure of a woman, if I do say so myself."

"Go admire it in the mirror in your room," Fargo said coldly.

"My, my," Janet said. "Are you sure that you're the real article? The famous Trailsman is supposed to bed every lady he meets, not boot them out of his room in the middle of the night."

There were times when Fargo sorely wished he did not have a reputation. "The famous Trailsman has already bedded one tonight and has no interest in bedding another."

Janet's smile evaporated and her face hardened. •
"Already bedded one? Who was it?"

"None of your damn business." Fargo gestured.
"Get up and get dressed. I have a long day ahead of
me tomorrow and I need some sleep."

"Was it Clarice? Has the tart thrown herself at you?
Or was it that hypocrite Millicent?"

"Get up," Fargo repeated.

"I demand to know," Janet snapped. "They're my
daughters."

Fargo couldn't resist. "I wouldn't know it from the
way you treat them."

"Is that so?" Janet said. "The mean-spirited mother
picking on her young, innocent daughters, is that how
you think of me?" She snorted. "You haven't seen
them as they truly are. You haven't had to put up
with years of their abuse."

"*They* abuse *you*?" Fargo said skeptically.

"In more ways than you can imagine. They have no
respect for me. None whatsoever. They talk back, they
insult me, they refuse to do as I ask them. So don't
expect me to be polite to them."

"You're not polite to anyone." Fargo folded his
arms, growing impatient for her to leave.

"Oh. So now it's me as a person." Janet made no
attempt to slide out from under the covers or to reach
for the robe that she had hung over the chair. "You
just don't like me, is that it?" Her mouth became a
slit. "Who are *you* to judge someone? From what I've
heard and read, you're hardly a paragon of virtue."

"Get up," Fargo said for the last time.

"You'll hear me out, damn it," Janet said. "Have
the decency to do that much if you're going to insult
a person!" She took a deep breath. "My life has been
a living hell from the moment I said 'I do.' I was
shocked to discover I married a weakling. A man with
no grit. A man who couldn't make up his mind if his

life depended on it. A man who wasn't really a man in the true sense of the word."

"I don't want to hear this."

"Why not? Does the truth make you squirm? How about when you learn that Desmond pampered our children to the point they became spoiled brats? How about the fact that wonderful little Clarice has slept with almost as many men as you have with women? Or that Millicent thinks she walks on water?"

"All I care about is the job," Fargo said.

"Which you only took to spite me," Janet reminded him. "Clarice and Millicent think it so gallant of you. They can't stop talking about their marvelous knight in shining armor." She dripped scorn from every pore.

"I'm no better than anyone else."

"You can say that again," Janet said. "And I'm no worse. I've done what I had to because I had no choice. Some people have accused me of wearing the pants in the family, but when the man refuses to wear them, what's a wife to do?"

"I never met your husband," Fargo said.

"Implying he might be different than how I paint him? Implying I'm lying?" Janet did not hide her resentment. "I can't say much for your bedside manner."

Fargo unfolded his arms and took a step toward the bed. He had tolerated as much as he was going to. But she wasn't looking at him anymore; she was staring inward.

"You have no idea of the torment I've been through. Desmond always asking me what I thought. Should we do this or should we do that."

"Some women would be happy their husband asked their opinion."

"It wasn't opinions he wanted, it was decisions," Janet said. "I had to make up my mind for both of us." She stopped and sighed. "Not an hour after we were wed, he came up to me and asked if I would mind if we lived with his mother for a year or so until we were ready to live on our own. His *mother*."

Fargo stopped by the bed but did not reach for her.

"I told him in no uncertain terms that we were adults and we would live on our own, and do you know what he did? He sulked the rest of the night. Our wedding night! He sulked and wouldn't touch me. But the worst was yet to come." Janet bowed her chin. "We had never been intimate. In my day it just wasn't done. Oh, we kissed a lot and cuddled a lot, but never *that*. So when he actually got around to doing it, I was set for the experience of my life. And do you know what happened?"

"No," Fargo said.

"It was like making love to a fish. There was no real passion. Oh, he kissed and cuddled just fine. But when it came to the actual act, he might as well have poked a goat. He got it over with and that was that. All in about a minute. I thought maybe he was nervous, but no, he always made love the same way. He would do it and roll over and go right to sleep, leaving me frustrated and unhappy."

"Some men are like that." Fargo had never quite understood how they could be, but he had heard they were.

"You're making excuses for him," Janet said. "But there is no justifying what Desmond did. I suffered. I suffered horribly, as surely as if he had taken a dagger and plunged it in my heart." She crossed her arms across her breasts. "Year after year of no passion. Year after year of being trapped in a marriage to a weakling."

So she turned to liquor, Fargo realized, and eventually to other men. Suddenly he did not dislike her nearly as much. "I'm sorry."

Janet's head snapped up. "Spare me your pity. I make no apologies for how I've lived my life. I've done what I've done in order to keep my sanity."

Janet paused, then asked in a small voice, "You're not going to make love to me, are you?"

"Not tonight," Fargo said.

Grasping at the straw, Janet brightened. "But you might another time? Very well. I'll hold you to that." She boldly threw off the quilt, slid off the bed, and picked up her robe.

Fargo had to give her credit. She was indeed a fine figure of a woman. Her breasts were full and curved upward at the tips, her belly was smooth, her legs were creamy and unblemished. She had the body of a woman half her age.

"Like what you see?" Janet teased. "Don't deny it. I can see it in your eyes." She slid into the robe but left it parted, exposing her breasts. Sashaying up to him, she crooked a finger under his chin. "And to think. All this could have been yours to do with as you please." Laughing, she moved to the door and glanced over her shoulder. "No hard feelings, I hope?"

"No hard feelings," Fargo said, and meant it.

"Then this hasn't been a total loss." Janet winked and went out, quietly shutting the door behind her.

"Well," Fargo said, and lay on the bed on his back. He did not bother to undress. He was too tired. But he could not stop thinking about Janet, about the life she had led. He had misjudged her, misjudged her badly. Granted, he only had her antics to go by, but as she said, that was just an excuse.

Sleep snuck up on him and the world darkened. Fargo's last thought before drifting off was that he should get up and blow out the lamp. How long he slept he couldn't say but suddenly his eyes were open again and he was straining to catch the sound that had awakened him. He did not have to strain hard.

Someone pounded on the door and a familiar voice called out, "Are you in there, hoss, or not?"

Sluggishly, Fargo rose on his elbows and swallowed

the cotton in his mouth. His window shade was framed by darkness. "Elias?"

The door opened and the old scout bounded in. "I've got news, son. News I reckoned you would want to hear right away."

"What time is it?" Fargo asked, rubbing his eyes.

"The sun will be up in half an hour and here you are sleepin' your life away." Elias shook his head but he was grinning. "Up late, were you, indulgin' in your favorite pastime?"

"You said something about news."

"Ever notice how some folks are grumps in the mornin'?" Dover snickered, then turned somber. "The Renegade has struck again. Two prospectors just brought in a body. Or what's left of it."

Fargo was off the bed before his friend finished. "Where are they now?"

"Over to the general store. The jasper who owns it also hires out as an undertaker. If you hurry we can see the carcass before they plant it."

"What's their rush?" Fargo asked as he trailed Elias out and turned to lock the door.

"Bodies tend to get a mite ripe in the heat," Elias said, "and this one is powerful whiffy already. He was killed three days ago."

The lobby was deserted and no one was at the front desk. A few people were astir in the street, early risers mostly, including a man sweeping a boardwalk and a woman hanging laundry out to dry.

A small crowd had gathered at the general store. Some were half dressed. All gazed grimly at the body, or what was left of it, that lay on a dirty canvas in the street. Two downcast dirty men with straggly whiskers stood on either side.

"Did you know him?" Fargo asked as he sank to a knee.

"Sure did," one of the prospectors answered. "He was our partner. Isaiah Redding, out of Illinois."

"He went off by himself to check a dry wash we came across," the other prospector said, "and when he didn't make it back for supper, we went to find out why."

"We warned him not to stray off alone," the other related, "but he always was a stubborn cuss. Now look. Whoever did this to him ain't hardly human."

Isaiah Redding could have died from any number of wounds. His throat had been slit from ear to ear. He had been stabbed repeatedly in the chest, right over the heart. He also had a knife wound in the head, and some of his brain matter had oozed out and dried around the edges. But the worst was his face. The Renegade had cut off Redding's nose. One ear was missing, the other had been sliced down the middle. Both eyes had been gouged out. The mouth was agape, revealing that the tongue was gone. The upper lip was intact but the lower lip hung by a shred.

"I can forget breakfast," someone in the crowd commented.

No one laughed.

Fargo bent closer. All of Redding's fingers had been chopped off but not the thumbs. Redding's footwear was gone, including his socks if he had any, and his toes had received the same treatment, except for the big toes. "Where are the missing parts?"

"They weren't anywhere around," one of Redding's friends responded. "We looked and looked, too."

"I don't know as I'd want to find that," the other said, and pointed at the deceased's groin.

Redding's manhood was gone. His pants had been slit open and his genitals sliced off, or almost. Part of the left testicle was still attached.

"Stinkin' Apaches," someone spat. "They should be rounded up and exterminated, the whole lot of 'em."

"How can anyone do this to another human being?" a woman asked no one in particular.

Fargo had seen worse. "What about his guns?"

"Guns?" the taller of the two prospectors repeated.

"Didn't he own a rifle or a pistol?" Fargo couldn't see anyone traipsing off into the mountains without one.

"Oh. Isaiah's long gun is on our packhorse. He never carried a revolver, though. He wasn't much of a shot."

The second prospector nodded. "He was always jokin' about how he couldn't hit the broad side of a barn even if it was close enough to touch it."

Apaches never passed up a weapon, although Fargo supposed that a lone warrior who already had a rifle had no real reason to take another. "Was anything else missing? Anything at all?"

"Not that we could see, no," the tall prospector said.

"His poke and tobacco pouch were still on him," the other revealed.

Fargo glanced at Elias, then stood. "Tell me where you found him. Or better yet, draw me a map."

"What for? You're not fixin' to go after the Renegade, are you?" the tall one asked. "Mister, that's plumb crazy. You'll end up like poor Isaiah."

But they drew the map Fargo wanted on a piece of paper provided by the owner of the general store. Fargo questioned them at length about landmarks to be sure he located the exact spot.

"But I still say you're loco," the tall one concluded. "I've learned my lesson. I'm leavin' for St. Louis just as soon as I can sell my pick and pan and whatnot. I'd rather be poor and breathin' than turned into one of them Turkish eunuchs."

"What's a eunuch?" the other one asked.

"Don't you know nothin'? A eunuch is a harem guard."

"What's a harem?"

Fargo drew the store owner aside and asked if the

man would open the store early so he could buy the few supplies he needed.

"Hellfire, mister, if you're going after the Renegade, you can have what you need free, and welcome to it. That murderin' redskin killed my younger brother four months ago. I'd go after him myself but I wouldn't last a week in the wilds. I'm a city boy."

An hour after daybreak Fargo and Elias Dover were ready. On the way out of Gila Bend Fargo made it a point to draw rein at the hitch rail in front of the restaurant. "I won't be long."

"If it's pie you're after, bring me a slice," Elias said. "If it's the redhead I hear tell you're sparkin', give her a kiss for me."

Fargo looked up from under the overhang. "Where did you hear about her?"

"You forget how much folks like to gossip," Elias bantered. "If this town had a newspaper, you would be front page news."

As usual, the tables, even at that early hour, were jammed from end to end. Maxine came out of the back carrying a tray laden with plates heaped with eggs and bacon and flapjacks. Her hair was up in a bun and she was wearing an apron. "Skye! This is a surprise. I haven't stopped thinking about you since last night."

"I'm on my way out of town," Fargo explained, "after the Renegade."

Maxine blanched, then said, "Don't move. I'll be right back." She bustled to the tables and returned with the empty tray. Snagging his sleeve, she pulled him into the kitchen and over to a corner as far from Sam and the stove as they could go.

"I heard about the latest killing. Must you do this? Can't you let someone else deal with it?"

The worry in her eyes was genuine and heartfelt. Fargo placed a hand on her shoulder and reminded her yet again, "No strings."

Maxine stiffened, then said curtly, "You can't fault a person for caring." She started to walk off but turned and planted a kiss full on his mouth. "There," she said. "Something to remember me by while the Renegade is cutting you into little pieces." Off she went, her posterior swaying.

Elias Dover was wearing a lopsided grin when Fargo emerged. "Did she get all mushy?"

"Go to hell."

"I'll take that as a yes. That's what happens when you let a pretty dress turn your head. Next thing, you walk out of restaurants lookin' as if you ate something that disagreed with you."

Fargo was sure he did not look like that at all but he did not make an issue of it. Mounting, he rode down the street and swung north once they were past the last of the buildings. Several well-defined trails led into the Gila Mountains. He chose the one the prospectors had told him to pick and for the next few hours wound steadily deeper and gradually higher into the stark range. By noon they came to a creek that only flowed a few months of the year, and followed it to the northwest.

Here and there they came upon prospectors, many of whom eyed them suspiciously with rifles at the ready.

About fifteen miles from town, in a narrow valley, the Halfway Camp, as it was called, had sprung up, a collection of tents clustered close together for mutual protection in case of a raid by the Apaches. In one of the tents a man who worked for the owner of the general store in Gila Bend sold items the prospectors would need but might not be inclined to travel all the way to town to buy. In another tent, a young man who worked at the Gila Bend saloon was doing a brisk business in hard liquor.

Fargo was surprised at how many prospectors were at the camp. There had to be four or five dozen. When he commented on it, the young man selling the liquor, whose name was Slim, handed him his drink, and nodded.

"This always happens right after a killing. They get scared. But it's been a few days, and by tonight I imagine most will be back at their claims."

"It's sure good for business," Fargo observed.

Slim lowered his voice. "Between you and me, mister, I'd just as soon that damned Renegade was six feet under. I get paid the same whether I serve ten drinks an hour or a hundred and I'd rather serve ten."

At least he was honest about his laziness. "Are there some who stay out at their claims and never come in?"

"Oh, sure. Some wouldn't leave if a whole tribe of Apaches was after them. All they care about is the silver."

Fargo was about to turn when he thought of another question he needed to ask. "Ever see three men called Spack, Toad and Grub?"

"Amos Spack? Sure. He's up this way quite a bit," Slim said. "He likes to fleece the silver hounds at cards."

"Does he have a claim of his own?"

"Not that I've heard about, no," Slim said. "He's not the kind to sweat for a living, if you get what I mean."

"Thanks," Fargo said. He polished off his whiskey and was stepping through the tent flap when Elias Dover poked him in the back.

"What was that about Spack? Do you reckon he's the one who took those shots at you in town?"

"Or one of his shadows," Fargo said. The assassin he had chased at the boardinghouse had been too big to be Spack.

"How do they fit into this whole business?" Dover asked.

"I'm not sure yet."

From the camp they rode north. Fargo constantly scoured for sign, and there was plenty. Horse tracks abounded, but every last one was shod. Toward sunset they stopped for the day and Fargo kindled a small fire and put a pot of coffee on. His meal consisted of pemmican.

Elias Dover sat cross-legged across from him, tamping tobacco into a pipe. Some fell over the side but he did not seem to notice. "I do so love the wilds," he remarked. "It will be a shame to have to give them up."

"You have ten or more good years left before you're ready for a rocking chair," Fargo said.

"Would that—" Elias stopped and gazed about them. "Do you ever wonder how it will be with you?"

"I don't expect to live that long," Fargo confessed. Not that he would mind if he did, but he couldn't buck the odds forever. No one did. The longer he stayed on the frontier, the less likely he would live to old age. But the wild places were in his blood. He could no more forsake them than he could stop breathing.

"We never know," Elias said. "We think we have it all worked out and life rears up and punches us in the gut to prove us wrong."

"The army firing you must have been quite a punch."

"Eh? Oh, that," Elias said in disgust. "It was just the latest in a string. But I'll get by. I always do whatever it takes."

Fargo chewed a while before saying, "When did your eyes start to go?"

Elias Dover had taken a brand from the fire and was about to light his pipe. He froze, but only for a few seconds. "How long have you known?"

"I didn't until just now."

"Then how—" Elias had forgotten about the pipe and dropped the brand into the flames.

"Colonel Patterson would never let go of a scout as good as you without a reason. No matter how old they were."

"What else?"

"Max told me that you fed her a yarn about not being able to read, and had her read the menu to you. Just now, when you were filling your pipe, you dropped tobacco and didn't see it." Fargo shrugged. "There were other little things."

"Damn. I thought I covered myself pretty well." Elias rested his elbows on his knees and his chin in his hands. "I can't see close up anymore, hoss. Far off, I'm fine. But if you were to wink at me right now, I wouldn't be able to tell."

"You shouldn't be here," Fargo said.

"I *have* to be here," Elias disagreed. "I need the money, need it like I've never needed anything in my life. Please, pard. I'm beggin' you."

Fargo frowned in embarrassment. "Stop it."

"If you cut me loose I'll go after the Renegade on my own," Elias vowed. "I tried once and couldn't catch him because of my bad eyes but with your help it will be a cinch." He clasped his hands in appeal. "Are we still in this together?"

Every now and then Fargo had an urge to beat his head against a tree. He had such an urge now. "We're still in it together."

Elias Dover beamed. "Thanks. You won't regret it. Wait and see."

"I hope to hell you're right."

8

Bloodstains were everywhere. Dark, broad stains where the prospector had his throat slit and the blood pooled under the body. Spatter marks where drops had fallen as various parts were cut or hacked. The stains would be there a good long while, until the rains in the fall, the lingering legacy of a man's life, the only legacy other than the dubious distinction of having been killed by the notorious Renegade.

That was the way of things west of the Mississippi. No man knew when his time would come, but come it often did, and violently, because violent death and the West went hand in hand. But that was to be expected in a land where tribes like the Apaches roamed wild and unbowed and resentful of the white men who wanted to tame all tribes and make them bow to white civilization and all it stood for.

Fargo did not want the West despoiled as the East had been. He did not care to see tribes like the Apaches and the Sioux caged in reservations. But neither could he stand for the wholesale slaughter of whites, or outright butchery, and the death of the prospector was butchery of the worst kind. Far worse than was customary even for Apaches. Sure, Apaches tortured their victims on occasion, but never like this. They didn't cut a man up into a hundred pieces. Once an enemy was dead, they tended to lose interest in the remains.

Yet Fargo found enough footprints and partial prints to tell beyond any shade of doubt that the killer wore Apache moccasins. No two tribes fashioned their footwear the same. Apache moccasins were different from Navajo moccasins and both were different from Pima and Maricopa moccasins. These were Apache.

The ground was rocky, the soil hard, so Fargo could not reconstruct the sequence of events as fully as he would have liked. He found where the killer had spied on the prospector from a vantage point higher up. The tracks told him that at one point the prospector had knelt and chipped away at an outcropping, and it was then the Renegade snuck from cover and descended without making a sound and came up behind the prospector and slit his throat before the man knew what struck him. Then all the Renegade had to do was stand back and wait for the blood to stop gushing and the prospector to stop thrashing.

It was only a guess, but Fargo believed the prospector had still been alive when his nose and ears and tongue were removed. The man had probably still been breathing when the Renegade chopped off his fingers and toes. The stab wounds, the fatal wounds, came later, after the Renegade had tired of inflicting torment.

The Renegade had gone off on foot. The trail was days old but Fargo could read even the faintest of sign like most men read a book, and soon he was bearing to the southwest on foot, leading the Ovaro by the reins.

Elias Dover followed on horseback, his rifle in hand. He was in a talkative mood. "It's awful not being able to track anymore. You have no idea."

"I have some," Fargo said without taking his eyes off the ground.

"Trackin' is my life. But now I couldn't track a bull buffalo if I was only five minutes behind it," the old scout lamented. "I can't see the damn tracks."

"You could hire out as a guide," Fargo suggested. "You know this country better than anyone."

"I know a lot of it," Elias agreed. "And truth to tell, I've been thinkin' about doin' just that. But I need some money to tide me over. That's why I went after the Renegade by my lonesome."

"You were lucky you weren't killed."

"I can still shoot, thank you," Elias said testily. "And I can see at a distance, remember? It's only up close I'm worthless."

"It's up close he'll slit your throat," Fargo said. Which he should keep in mind, himself.

"If I die, I die," Elias said philosophically. "But I'm not about to spend the rest of my days in a hotel room because I'm too scared to face the outside world."

"I never claimed you would," Fargo said. "Don't put words in my mouth."

"I can't help being touchy. My whole life has turned upside down. I'm not the man I used to be and I have to face that fact and live accordingly," Elias said. "And I do mean *live*. Witherin' away in a rockin' chair ain't for me."

It wasn't for Fargo, either. "Buffalo hunts on the plains are popular with those with money," he mentioned. "You could do well."

"Nursemaid a bunch of greenhorns," Elias said in mild disgust. "Is that what I've been reduced to? If I had a thimble full of sand I'd slit my own throat."

"Running from a problem never solves it."

"Easy for a man to say when he has the eyes of an eagle," Elias responded. "We take too much for granted and don't miss it until we lose it."

They came to a stretch of solid rock and the sign disappeared. While Elias held the Ovaro's reins, Fargo roved in ever wider circles. There had to be sign some-

94

where. But although he searched and searched, especially where the rock merged with softer soil, he could not find so much as a heel print.

"He's crafty, this Renegade," Elias Dover said. "Folks say he's not entirely human, that he's a ghost in human form."

"Folks say a lot of dumb things," Fargo replied. One of the dumbest was that Indians were animals who should be exterminated like vermin.

"I'm only sayin' how it is. I didn't say I agreed." Elias brought the Ovaro up for him to climb on. "Where to now?"

"We keep looking."

"Whatever you want, but the Renegade is long gone by now. We have a better chance of findin' a needle in a haystack."

"Give up if you want." Fargo wouldn't rest until he brought the killer to bay, however long it took.

"There you go again," Elias complained. "And you say *I* put words in *your* mouth? I'm in this to the end, pard."

"What we need is high ground," Fargo said. "The highest we can find." A peak to the southeast appeared to qualify. They spent the rest of the afternoon reaching and climbing it. The upper slopes were treacherous. Steep, and littered with talus, they nonetheless afforded a sweeping vista of the surrounding countryside.

"You think this will do?" Elias asked.

"If it doesn't, we have to wait for the Renegade to strike again," Fargo said.

"It usually happens in clusters. There will be three or four in a row, then nothing for a while. He must rest up between attacks. Maybe he goes back to his wickiup and the wife and kids."

"Could be," Fargo said. It could also be the Renegade was a loner and the rest of the tribe had no idea what he was up to. Although by now word was bound to have trickled to the Chiricahuas and Mimbres that one of their own might be wreaking a fearsome vengeance on the hated whites.

To the west a bloodred sun was on the verge of relinquishing the heavens. A few clouds, reflecting the glow, drifted like floating crimson pillows.

Elias Dover breathed deep and said, "When my time comes I want to be planted and left to rot."

"I was thinking of feeding you to coyotes."

"That's not what I meant. No coffin. No funeral. No pretendin' I've mattered or that anyone cares. Dust to dust does me fine."

"Let's not get ahead of ourselves," Fargo advised. "You'll outlive me and look back on this one day and laugh."

"I never laugh about dyin'," Elias said. "It's too permanent."

Twilight fell, cloaking the mountains in deepest shadows. The shadows spread and merged, transforming into a veil of darkness. One by one points of light appeared both in the sky and sprinkled about the countryside.

Elias went to his horse and opened his saddlebags. He came back wagging a flask. "To keep the chill out." Opening it, he offered first swallow to Fargo. "Do you really reckon this will work?"

The whiskey seared a pleasant path to Fargo's gut, washing down a lot of dust. "It might," he coughed. "Any fire smaller than the rest could be the Renegade's, and we'll have him."

Indians generally made smaller campfires than whites. It was plain common sense. Small fires were less likely to be spotted by an enemy. Some white men made fires that could be seen in the next territory.

Fargo studied the scores below with interest. Those closest to the horizon he ignored. He was more interested in campfires in the immediate vicinity, and there were plenty. The mountains crawled with prospectors.

"Look at 'em all," Elias marveled.

Fargo counted over twenty within five miles of the mountain. All big and bright. None a fire an Apache would make. "We'll give it more time," he said, passing back the flask.

Elias chugged and smacked his lips and wiped his mouth with his sleeve. "Beats a fire all hollow." He twisted to gaze to one side and then the other. "I've never been this high up in the Gilas at night. It's right pretty. Like when I was a boy back in Ohio and the fireflies came out at night."

"You're getting poetical in your old age."

"Go to hell." Elias swallowed more whiskey. "It's hell addin' wrinkles, hoss. Inside you're still that boy back in Ohio but your body is a bundle of aches and pains." He looked at Fargo. "I got old by accident. But if I had it to do again, I'd try a little harder to die a little younger."

"You've had too much to drink," Fargo said.

"Like hell I have." Elias imbibed a bit more to prove it. "Poke fun if you want but it's a terrible thing to have all your vinegar and vim drain away year by year to where when you wake up in the mornin', your joints crack and pop and won't hardly work."

"I'll remember that." Fargo was scanning the campfires.

"No you won't," Elias said. "At your age, old age is so far off, you ignore it. It's something that happens to other folks, it won't really happen to you. But it will. And you'll look back and wish you listened to me."

Was it a trick of Fargo's eyes, or was there a small orange dot to the southwest? He leaned forward, straining to see it better.

"That's the way it always is, the way it's always been," Elias rambled on. "By the time we've lived long enough to know what's what, we're ready for the grave. It's a shame. It should be the other way around.

97

We should start out wise as owls and get stupid as we get older."

"Some do," Fargo absently remarked.

"I took the wrong trail so many times," Elias said. "I'd like to help you so you don't make the same mistakes but the only way to learn they are mistakes is to make them. If that makes any kind of sense."

"Put that flask away before I have to carry you to your horse."

"Have I told you to go to hell recently?" Elias grinned.

By now Fargo was certain. It *was* a small fire, about three miles off as the crow flew, maybe five on horseback although distances were difficult to determine at night. "There," he said, and pointed.

"Could be," Elias conceded after a while. "Could not be, too."

"Only one way to find out." Rising, Fargo took hold of the Ovaro's reins and started down on foot.

"I was hopin' for a good night's sleep," Elias mentioned, doing the same. "We'll be lucky to turn in before midnight."

"Think of your half of the reward," Fargo said. "That should inspire you."

"You have no idea," Elias responded. "When you have barely ten dollars to your name, five hundred is a fortune."

"No amount of money is worth dying over." Fargo was not one of those willing to sacrifice his life for simple greed.

"It depends on how empty your belly is," Elias allowed. "Or how much you'd like a roof over your head. Me, I've grown right fond of wakin' up in a soft bed. Sleepin' on the ground is a lot harder on the back."

"You're growing soft," Fargo teased.

"At my age who can blame me? I'm entitled, damn it. But because I was dumb as a stump when I was your age, I never planned ahead. So here I am, waltzin' around in the dark, liable to break my leg if not my fool neck, just so I can get enough money to go on sleepin' in warm beds a while."

Somewhere to the west a coyote yipped and was answered by another to the north.

"I'll miss it when I go," Elias said. "Hell, I miss it already."

"One minute you need money to sleep in warm beds the rest of your life, the next you're in the grave. Make up your mind."

Elias laughed. "Your turn will come. When it does, I honestly hope you're braver or smarter than I ever was. That's what it takes. Courage or brains. Have both and you can have anything."

They came to where the ground leveled and climbed on their horses. From then on neither said a word until hours later when they drew rein on a ridge overlooking the fire Fargo had spotted from up high, and this close it was still a small fire, still the kind of fire an Indian would make. Still the kind of fire Apaches favored.

"How do we get down there without givin' ourselves away?" Dover whispered.

The campfire was in a canyon with high walls and there appeared to be only one way in or out. A box canyon, raising doubts in Fargo's mind. "No Apache would trap himself like that."

"Maybe it's a dumb one," Elias said.

"You have dumb on the brain tonight," Fargo chided, and swung down. "Stay here and watch the horses. I'll fire twice into the air if it's safe to bring them down."

"Why you and not me?" the old scout demanded. "I can be as quiet as you."

"You can't see a twig in front of you. I can," Fargo gave it to him honestly. He shucked the Henry from his saddle scabbard and fed a cartridge into the chamber. If you don't hear the signal in an hour, head for Gila Bend."

"I've never run from a scrape and I'm too old to start," Elias said. "If I don't hear from you in an hour, it will be my turn."

"Has anyone ever told you that your head is made of petrified wood?" Fargo once had a piece he picked up in the redwood country of northern California.

"My mother used to say I had granite between my ears," Elias said. "Claimed I took after my father."

Fargo smiled and bent down and removed his spurs. Apaches had keener ears than most, and although his spurs rarely jangled when he did not want them to, he put them in his saddlebags, then dropped over the rim, padding softly, careful not to dislodge loose pebbles and dirt.

The canyon mouth was wide enough for several Conestogas to enter abreast. Sticking to the darkest patches, Fargo crept along the north wall until he rounded a bend and saw the campfire clearly. Disappointment knifed through him. From up on the mountain the fire had appeared to be small but it was a big fire, a white man's fire. Thanks to the high canyon wall, only part of it had been visible.

In confirmation came voices, white voices. Fargo went far enough to spy four prospectors hunkered in for the night, drinking coffee and joking and laughing. He did not reveal himself to them.

The fatigue Fargo had been fighting off could not be denied any longer. It had been a long, hard day, and he was tired. He retraced his path to the crest of the ridge and without saying anything shoved the Henry into the scabbard.

"So what now?" Elias Dover asked.

"We wait for the Renegade to strike again." Fargo's saddle creaked as he tiredly stepped into the stirrups.

"All the way to town?" Elias asked. "Or Halfway Camp?"

"The camp."

It was four in the morning before they got there. The tents stood quiet and dark. Fargo drew rein near the makeshift saloon, stripped the Ovaro, spread out his bedroll, and was asleep within seconds of his head hitting the saddle.

Ordinarily, Fargo was up before first light and today was no exception. Only this time he had a dog to thank. Its barking roused him from the bottom of a well. His eyelids leaden, he sat up and blinked and saw that the eastern horizon was framed by a bright pink band.

"Damned dogs." Elias Dover had already woken. His hat was beside him and he was scratching his head and yawning. "But I suppose I should be grateful. I can have breakfast that much sooner." He produced the flask, enjoyed a swig, then held it out.

"I'll wait and have coffee," Fargo said. He was as much a drinking man as anyone, but whiskey for breakfast was overdoing it.

"When your joints ache as much as mine, bug juice gets you on your feet faster," Elias said.

The camp was rousing to life. Men were coming out of tents, rising from under blankets, washing in the stream. Fargo shuffled to a gravel bar, sank onto his hands and knees, and plunged his head in the ice-cold water. It did what whiskey and coffee could never do: it instantly woke him up.

Shivering, Fargo tossed his head back and forth to shed the excess, then donned his hat and stood.

Elias was watching in amusement and sipping from the flask. "Do that again. It gave me gooseflesh just to watch."

"How about if I throw you in and give you more?" Fargo set to saddling the Ovaro, then led it around to the front of the saloon tent. "I wonder if we can get a meal around here?" No sooner were the words out of his mouth than the tantalizing aroma of frying bacon tingled his nose and caused his stomach to growl like a famished wolverine's.

Elias sniffed a few times, and pointed. "That way."

The flaps to a large tent had been tied back. Inside was a long table, a stove, and a stout woman with ruddy cheeks, her gray hair in a bun, doing double duty as cook and waitress.

"What will it be?" she greeted Fargo and Elias as they sat down. "We have eggs and bacon or bacon and eggs."

Fargo grinned. "I was hoping for eggs with bacon or bacon with eggs."

The woman had nice even teeth. "If I were ten years younger and single I could take a shine to you."

"I'm available," Elias said.

"You're married to the bottle," the stout woman said. "I can smell it on your breath." She wagged a thick finger at him. "You should be ashamed, a man your age." Off she went to greet new arrivals.

Elias stared after her. "I think I'm in love."

"A man your age," Fargo mimicked her.

"I'm goin' blind, I ain't dead," was Elias' comment. He could not take his eyes off the matron. "I always did like women with big hips. It comes from being raised on a farm and watchin' the cows."

Fargo did not see how that was a factor and he was not about to ask.

In short order the woman brought them heaping plates of scrambled eggs and bacon, each with a side of toast. She poured a cup of coffee for Fargo and a cup for Elias, and added a spoonful of sugar to Elias'.

"For my special customers," she said sweetly, and was gone.

Fargo thought his friend's lower jaw would fall off. "Is that your secret for attracting the ladies? You drool over yourself?"

"Go to hell."

"Where have I heard that before?"

The eggs were hot, the bacon crisp, the coffee as good as coffee ever got. Their bill came to sixty cents.

"It's highway robbery," Elias complained, the luster gone from his budding romance.

"At least she didn't charge us for wiping up the drool."

The saloon tent was open but Fargo still felt it was too early and made a circuit of the camp. There was not much to see. Tents and more tents and horses and men as rough and dirty as the mountains around them.

"Reckon we can find a poker game to sit in on?" Elias speculated.

Fargo wouldn't mind. But they were denied the opportunity. Out of the north galloped two frantic prospectors leading a third horse to which another prospector had been tied. The third man was alive, but barely. They reined up in a cloud of dust and others rushed to help them lower their stricken companion onto a blanket. The stout woman from the cook tent came to tend him, and recoiled, aghast.

Fargo did not blame her. The victim was the same as the rest. His nose had been cut off. His ears were missing. His mouth was a welter of drying blood, his tongue a stump. Several fingers on his left hand were gone. Those on his right had not been touched. His throat had been slit, but not deeply. The Renegade had botched it, for once, and the prospector was still alive. But he wouldn't be for long.

"Where did this happen?" Fargo asked the pair who had brought him in.

"At our claim," one answered. "We have a dugout we sleep in. Made it after the killings started so we could sleep safe at night. Sam, here, went out about midnight and off into the bushes. When he didn't come back, we went looking and saw the Renegade bent over him."

Fargo gripped the prospector by the shoulders. "You actually saw who did it? What did he look like?"

"It was a big Indian with a big knife," the prospector said. "I didn't see his face that good. He was helpin' himself to Fred's poke. But he had long hair like an Apache and a breechcloth like Apaches wear, and moccasins."

"Tell me where to find your claim."

The dugout was only three miles from Halfway Camp. Fargo found the spot in the bushes with no problem. The blood was dry but bright red. He stood over the fresh prints in the soft soil and said more to himself than to Elias, "I'll be damned."

"What?" the old scout asked.

"The Renegade's tracks," Fargo said. "They're twice the size of those we saw yesterday."

"How is that possible?"

It wasn't.

9

Not only were the tracks twice the size, the moccasins the killer wore were wider across the heel than across the instep. The previous tracks had been the opposite. Fargo bent closer, noting more details. The whole pattern was different. "These aren't real Apache moccasins. But someone wants us to think they are."

Elias absorbed that, then said, "Are you sayin' what I think you're sayin'?"

Uncoiling, Fargo roved in search of more sign. "The last attack, the killer didn't take the prospector's poke. This attack, the killer did."

"Now that I think about it," Elias mentioned, "it's been that way since near the beginnin'. Sometimes the pokes are missin', sometimes they're not."

"I've yet to meet an Apache who gives a damn about money," Fargo said.

"A white man would." Elias stared at the blood. "It would take the most devious bastard alive to do somethin' like this."

The tracks brought them to a gully where a horse had been hidden. The hoofprints were plain as could be.

"I'll be! It's shod," Elias said. "When the prospectors hear about this, there will be hell to pay."

"We're not going to tell them."

"We're not? Shouldn't they be warned?"

"They already know a killer is on the loose. So what if there are two killers?" Fargo shook his head. "We'll tell them after it's over. After we have it all worked out and the killers are belly down over a saddle."

"That could take a while," Elias observed.

"Not if I can help it." Fargo swung back onto the Ovaro and they were off again, following the gully to where the killer had headed practically due west at a gallop. After less than a mile the killer had stopped and climbed down. Fargo dismounted and hunkered.

"What was he up to?" Elias asked.

"He changed clothes." Fargo pointed at several partial tracks. "He switched his moccasins for boots."

"I'll be damned."

From there the killer had ridden south. Not long after he changed direction again.

"The polecat is circlin' back to the claim." Elias scratched his chin. "Why in tarnation would he do that?"

The tracks provided the answer. The killer hadn't circled to the claim, he had circled to the trail leading to Halfway Camp.

"He followed the prospectors when they took the body in," Fargo said.

"Then he could have been one of those standin' around when we were lookin' at it!" Elias declared.

"Unless he cut off the trail before he got there."

Which was exactly what the killer had done. Making no attempt to cover his tracks, the killer had gone into the hills to the northeast.

"How did you know?" Elias asked.

"His kind travel in packs," was all Fargo would say. They rode another half a mile. Past the hills were more mountains with timbered slope, and in a clearing by a spring five horses had been picketed. A fire was going. Two men lounged beside it. Neither showed any alarm when Fargo and Elias Dover entered the clearing.

Fargo had the Henry across his saddle. He drew rein several yards out and said matter-of-factly, "I knew it would be you."

"Light and sit a spell," Amos Spack said, motioning with his coffee cup. "I'm feelin' hospitable."

"You mangy coyote," Elias said.

"What do you have against coffee?" Spack asked him.

Toad smirked and flexed his big hands. "That was a good one, Amos. You always come up with good ones."

"You think this is funny, you big ox?" Elias snapped. He had his hand on his revolver. "I should shoot you where you sit."

"Hereabouts they call that murder," Spack said, and Toad roared.

Fargo did not like it. They were too smug, too confident. "Where's your other partner? Charlie Grub?"

"In good time," Spack said. "Climb down. The coffee ain't poisoned." At that Toad laughed anew.

"I don't drink with sidewinders," Elias informed him.

Fargo dismounted and let the reins dangle. He was watching the trees but he did not see anyone. He stood to one side of the fire so the pair couldn't jump him. With a start, he realized all five of the horses were saddled.

"I've been expectin' you," Amos Spack said.

"I figured as much." The horses worried Fargo more than Grub's absence. One was little more than a pony.

"You're supposed to be one of the best trackers alive," Spack was saying. "This was bound to happen."

"Trying to shoot me in town was what gave you away," Fargo mentioned.

Spack shrugged. "A man has to gamble sometimes. I nearly had you on the main street. You moved just as I squeezed the trigger."

"You admit it?" Elias Dover marveled.

"Why not?" Spack rejoined. "Fargo, here, knows what is going on even if you don't, old man."

Elias looked at Fargo. "What in hell is he jabberin' about?"

Before Fargo could answer, Amos Spack said, "It would be best all around if you two shed your hardware. The old coot might get the wrong notion and blaze away. And we wouldn't want that, would we?"

"No," Fargo said.

Elias glanced back and forth in confusion. "I'll be damned if I'll drop my guns so this sidewinder can blow out my wick. Give me one good reason why I should?"

"I'll give you two," Spack said, and hollered, "Charlie! Show our guests our little surprise."

From out of the pines strode the third hardcase, and he wasn't alone. Maxine Walters walked in front of him, pale as a sheet, an arm around Donny. Charlie Grub had a shotgun trained on their backs.

"You miserable sons of bitches," Elias fumed.

Toad slowly straightened. "I'm tired of you callin' us names, old man. One more time and you die where you sit."

Elias bristled. "I'd like to see you try."

"Now, now," Amos Spack said. "We wouldn't want any harm to come to the woman and her brat, would we? Or don't you care about them, old-timer? Your friend does. He cares about the female a lot. Just ask Grub. He was spyin' on them the other night and saw a show, let me tell you."

Fargo had never wanted to shoot anyone more than he wanted to shoot these three, but all he could do was stand there. "So that was Grub I swapped shots with near the river."

"Winged him, too," Amos revealed. "Made him mad as hell. He wanted to go back and strangle the woman and her boy to spite you but I convinced him they were more important to us alive." He was quite pleased with himself. "Not long after you rode out, we snatched the boy. Once she knew we had him, she came along as meekly as a lamb. Now here we are." Spack smiled at Maxine as she and Donny came to a halt. "It's been fun, hasn't it, sweetheart?"

"Has he touched you?" Fargo asked her.

"He's been a perfect gentleman," Maxine said bitterly. "Watched us like hawks day and night."

"I hate him," Donny declared. "I hate them all." He glared at Spack. "This one said if I didn't behave, he would hurt Ma."

"And I haven't laid a finger on her, have I, boy?" Amos Spack said. "So quit your bellyachin'." He nodded at Fargo, at the Henry. "I won't say it twice about the hardware. The old one is hot air but you're fast. You're dangerous."

Fargo avoided looking at Maxine as he tucked at the knees to lower the Henry to the ground.

"Don't!" she exclaimed. "Not for my sake! You know what he'll do!"

"Hush, woman," Spack said. "He has your best interests at heart. You should be grateful."

Fargo placed his Colt next to the Henry and straightened. Right away Toad came over and took them, chuckling all the while.

Elias had not moved. His mouth was twitching but he did not say anything, even when Spack gazed his way and arched an eyebrow.

"Well? What's it going to be, old man? Your pard rates the female higher than his own hide. How about you?"

"She's nothin' to me," Elias said.

"Is that a fact?" Spack tipped his cup to his lips. "Then I guess you won't object if I have Charlie blow her spine in two?"

"Do whatever you want," Elias said, with a lot less conviction. "But when he shoots, I'll put a slug into you."

"You're one tough hombre," Spack taunted. "But how about the boy? Ever seen a kid's innards splattered from here to hell and back again? That shotgun ain't loaded with rock salt."

Beads of sweat dotted Elias' brow. "You could do that?"

"Hell, old-timer, I've bucked out more folks than you have fingers and toes, in ways that would curdle your blood. Once there was a family in a wagon. Settlers who thought they could make it to Texas on their own. They were wrong." Spack smiled at the memory. "They had a baby. I tied it upside down from a tree and used it for target practice."

"I remember that," Toad said. "It got you mad, bawlin' like it was."

Maxine had regained some of her color. "You're despicable. All three of you deserve to hang."

"That we do," Spack cheerfully conceded. "But I aim to go on breathin' a good long while yet." To Charlie Grub he said, "If the old buzzard hasn't dropped his rifle and his belly gun by the time I count to five, shoot the bitch and her pup."

"You're bluffin'," Elias said.

Spack looked at Fargo. "Why did you let this old fart tag along? He's about to get all of you killed, and for what?" Spack paused, then said loudly, "One!"

"I mean it about puttin' a slug in you," Elias warned.

"Two!"

Fargo could not bring himself to ask Dover to give up his guns. He tensed, girding to spring at Toad and wrest the Henry from his grasp. He would do it when Spack reached four and try to save Max and Donny.

"Three!" Amos Spack called out. He was a cat sadistically toying with a mouse and he would win no matter what the mouse did.

Elias Dover was staring at Maxine but it dawned on Fargo the scout could not see her expression, could not see the fear in her eyes or how she clutched her son in rising dread of their imminent deaths. Then Elias suddenly thrust his arms out from his sides and hollered, "All right! You win! Don't hurt them."

Spack acted disappointed. "After all that bluster you folded without callin' my bluff? I'd like to play you at poker, old man. I'd clean you out in no time."

"You would try," Elias said, but the anger had drained out of him and he did not resist when Toad came over and relieved him of his guns.

"That's better," Spack said. "Now we can sit and talk all peaceable, like."

Fargo would just as soon stand but with the shotgun fixed on Maxine's back, he deemed it wiser to go along with Spack's whims for the time being. "What do we have to talk about?"

"For starters, whether you've told anyone about us." Spack flicked a finger at Toad and Grub. "If there's a lynch mob out to invite us to a strangulation jig, I'd as soon light a shuck for San Francisco."

"Taking the money and ore you've stolen with you," Fargo said.

"I didn't go to all this trouble only to leave it behind. We have pretty near seven thousand dollars. It's not exactly a fortune but with my share and a little luck at cards I can make it one."

"Which one of you kills the prospectors?" Not that it mattered. Fargo needed to keep Spack talking.

"Toad and Grub take turns. Toad did the honors last time. Charlie will do the next one."

"You don't help out?" Fargo glanced at Maxine, trying to get her attention, but she was staring at Spack.

"We've only got the one pair of moccasins and they don't fit me."

"Then who killed Isaiah Redding nearly a week ago? The tracks were smaller than Toad's and Grub's."

"Who else?" Spack said. "The Renegade." He snickered to himself. "Oh. I savvy. You think we've done all the killin'? I'd like to take the credit but I can't. The Renegade started it."

"So there really is a crazed Apache on the loose?" This from Elias. "You figure to have all the blame for your killin's heaped on his shoulders, and when you're ready, you and these other two lunkheads can ride out with no one guessin' the truth."

"You finally figured it out," Spack said. "A great brainstorm, if I do say so myself. It came to me after about the third killin' when someone mentioned that the Renegade never took anything from those he butchered. Only an Apache would be so stupid as to let all those coins and nuggets go to waste."

"So you made a pair of moccasins and began killing," Fargo said.

"The moccasins were the hard part," Spack said. "They had to be Apache or folks wouldn't be fooled. Then I heard of a Chiricahua who was shot down near the border, and we went and dug up the body."

"Lordy, it stank," Toad said.

"The moccasins weren't in very good shape but all I had to do was copy them close enough to pull the wool over everyone's eyes." Spack reached behind him and held up the moccasins for all to behold. "My pride and joys. I never stitched together anything in my life but they didn't turn out half bad."

"Once you had them, you would wait for the Renegade to strike, then murder a few prospectors for their pokes." Fargo had it all worked out.

"And the ones we killed were always blamed on

the Apache," Spack gloated, but then frowned. "Then you came along."

"Did you know who I was that first day on the trail?"

"No. I took a shine to that Henry of yours. I figured we would jump you and cut you up to make it look like the Renegade did it, but you snuck on past us. I knew you suspected we were fixin' to kill you, and I didn't want you tellin' anyone or folks might start to wonder."

"So you took those shots at me on the street."

"Later, afer we learned who you were, and that the Hammonds had hired you to find their father, I had even more cause to want you dead."

"Was it you who killed Desmond Hammond?" Fargo asked.

"I would have liked to. I don't much cotton to Easterners. But the Renegade has to take the credit."

"All this talk," Toad said.

"Be patient, damn you," Spack snapped. "We'll get to it in a minute. There's no rush. We have them over a barrel."

"You would like to think so," Fargo told him, "but you made two mistakes. Either can get you strung up."

Amos Spack sneered in disbelief. "Mistakes? This should be interestin'. Let me hear them."

"Your first mistake was having Toad and Grub wear the moccasins. They're twice as big as the Renegade and someone else besides me is bound to notice the tracks are different."

"So far no one has. People are a lot more stupid than you give them credit for being. What was my second mistake?"

"Taking Maxine and her son out of town in broad daylight. Someone was bound to notice. When they turn up missing, you'll be the first one to be questioned."

"Who will do the questionin'?" Spack responded. "She doesn't have a husband. She doesn't have any kin in Gila Bend. Oh, that bald cook might wonder where she got to, and maybe a few others, but they'll figure she finally saved up enough money and headed east as she's been sayin' she would do."

"You think you have it all worked out," Fargo said.

"I *know* I do," Spack confidently declared. "It's as perfect as can be. A few thousand more and we'll have ten grand. Six months from now I'll be sippin' fine whiskey in San Francisco and no one will ever know where I got the money to buy it."

"What about your partners?"

Spack visibly tensed. "What about them?"

"How much money do they get?"

It was Toad who answered. "Equal shares, mister. We're dividin' it into thirds and going our separate ways."

"Thirds?" Fargo repeated. "Let's see. A third of ten thousand would give each of you a little over three thousand dollars. That wouldn't last long in a city like San Francisco. I've been there."

Toad glanced at Charlie Grub, who said, "What are you gettin' at, mister?"

"Don't listen to him, boys," Spack said.

Fargo gestured. "All I'm saying is that fine whiskey doesn't come cheap. It costs a lot to live like a king. Three thousand dollars isn't enough. It wouldn't last three months."

"I told you," Spack said sourly, "I aim to win the rest I need at cards."

Fargo smiled at Toad and Grub. "Why would he risk his share in a poker game when there's a surer way for him to get his hands on a lot of money?"

"What way would that be?" Toad wasn't the sharpest knife around.

"He can take yours," Fargo said, and sensed he had

114

come close to the truth by the lurid curses that spewed from Amos Spack. "Ten thousand is a lot better than three thousand any day."

"Amos would never do that to us," Toad said.

Charlie Grub gnawed on his lower lip and dubiously regarded Spack. "It's strange, though, Toad. Remember that fella we ran into who said he knew Spack back when Spack had another partner by the name of Johnson. And how Johnson up and disappeared one day."

If looks could kill, Spack's would have shriveled Fargo where he sat. "I told you yacks before. Johnson is back in Indiana living with his folks."

"Could be he is," Charlie Grub said. "Could be he isn't. Could be we'd be smart to take our share of the money right now and hide it so only we know where it is."

"There's an idea," Toad said.

Spack gave an exaggerated shrug. "It's fine by me, boys. Why don't I give you all of the money to hold? Would that prove I'm not out to stab you in the back?"

"We never said you were, Amos." Toad sounded hurt by the accusation.

"It's what Charlie is implyin'," Spack said. "That I'm no good. That I killed my last partner and I plan to kill both of you once we have enough money."

"I didn't say any such thing," Grub argued. "All I said was that it wouldn't hurt to split the money we already have."

"It's the same damn thing," Spack said. "You don't trust me anymore. And all on account of a pack of lies from a man who wants to buck us out in gore."

"You can hold on to my share if you want," Toad offered.

"No," Spack said. "We'll do this right. We owe Charlie that much. Later he can say he's sorry and beg me to forgive him." Spack grinned but it was forced. "First, though, you know what to do with our guests."

Charlie Grub covered Fargo and Elias Dover. "Off that horse, old man. Lie on your backs with your arms and legs spread and be quick about it."

"The hell I will," the old scout said. And with that, with no forewarning, he hauled on his mount's reins. His dun reacted superbly and was all the way around and breaking into a gallop before the three cutthroats collected their wits about them.

"Shoot, damn it!" Amos Spack cried, leaping to his feet and drawing his short-barreled Smith and Wesson.

Fargo took a step but Toad aimed his own Colt at him and cocked it almost in his face.

"Stay right where you are."

By then Elias was at the edge of the clearing and bent low over his saddle horn to make it that much harder for Charlie Grub to hit him. Grub didn't try; he shot the dun instead.

A high-pitched whinny pierced the clearing as the horse buckled into a forward roll. Elias was catapulted from the saddle and struck the trunk of a pine with a sharp *crack*. His horse came to rest with its legs thrashing and blood gouting from its nostrils. It was lung shot and would not last long.

Fargo simmered with fury as Spack and Grub ran over and Amos Spack flipped Elias onto his back. The old scout was as limp as a wet rag. Squatting, Spack gripped Dover's chin and it drooped in his hand. When Spack let go, Elias' head flopped to one side, his eyes wide open but as blank as an empty slate.

"I'll be!" Charlie Grub exclaimed. "His neck is broke!"

"That it is," Spack confirmed, and laughed. "Convenient of him to kill himself and save us the trouble."

"Poor Mr. Dover," Maxine said softly, tears brimming her eyes. "He always treated me kindly."

Amos Spack did something completely uncalled for. He stood up and spat in the old scout's face. "That's for meddlin' where you shouldn't." Happy at the turn of events, he faced Fargo. "Now then. Where were we?" He snapped his fingers. "I remember. We were about to stake you out, Apache style."

"You can't," Maxine said.

"Haven't you been listenin', sweetheart?" Spack retorted. "I can do any damn thing I please, and it pleases me to have Mr. High-and-Mighty end his days as buzzard droppin's." He grinned in sadistic glee. "Let's get to it."

10

There was nothing Fargo could do. Amos Spack covered him while Toad and Charlie Grub threw his hat to the dirt and stripped off his shirt. Grub then tripped him. He sprawled onto his back and Grub fell on top of him, Grub's knee on his chest.

"Hold real still," Spack warned. "My trigger finger is itchin' to pull this trigger."

Toad disappeared for a bit and when he returned he carried four tent stakes and a large rock for pounding them into the ground. "All set, Amos," he announced. "Want me to do the honors?"

"Get it done."

Maxine clasped Donny in mute horror. "The Renegade has never staked anyone out before. People won't believe he did it."

"Apaches do it all the time," Spack shot back. "Besides, stakin' your lover out is just the beginnin'."

"How do you mean?"

"I like hurtin' things. I like makin' folks suffer." Spack licked his thin lips. "This tall drink of water will be a long time dyin'."

Toad came around and knelt on Fargo's left side.

He set the stakes and the rock down, placed a hand on Fargo's left wrist, and yanked to straighten Fargo's arm. He yanked so hard he nearly tore the arm from the socket. "I like hurtin' things too," he said.

"You're animals!" Maxine declared. "Filthy, depraved beasts. I hope they catch you and hang you like you deserve."

"Don't be callin' us names," Spack growled.

Toad placed a hand on a stake. "Yeah, not unless you want the same to happen to you and your brat, missy."

Spack glanced sharply at him. "Since when do you make the decisions? I'll decide what we do with them."

Maxine swallowed and said, "Threaten me all you want. You're still as vile as can be. I only wish I had a gun. I've never killed anyone but I would gladly kill pigs like you."

That was too much for Amos Spack. Whirling, he strode up to her and backhanded her across the face. Maxine was jarred backward. Donny, crying out, tore free of her grasp and launched himself at Spack.

Toad and Charlie Grub twisted to watch, and that was when Fargo struck. Wrenching free of Toad's hold on his wrist, he grabbed a stake, and as Toad shifted toward him, he thrust the tapered end of the stake into Toad's neck.

Horrified, Toad grabbed the stake and did the very thing he should not have done—he ripped it out, and shrieked.

Fargo bucked upward as blood sprayed on his hair and shoulders. Charlie Grubb was still looking at Spack and Maxine and had not realized what had happened until Toad shrieked. Bleating in surprise, Grub started to turn and clawed for his revolver.

Fargo's fingers found it first. A quick flick, and Fargo had the Remington in his hand. He jammed the muzzle against Grub's side and fired.

Howling, Grub fell to the right, pressing his hands to the wound. His legs were across Fargo's, and Fargo had to kick them off to rise. Fargo swung toward Amos Spack only to see the wily killer in full flight toward the horses. Instantly, Fargo took aim. Ordinarily he would not shoot a man in the back but in Spack's case he was glad to make an exception. But just as his finger tightened on the trigger, a wet hand seized his forearm and another clamped onto his throat. The Remington went off but the slug went wide instead of into Spack.

Toad's neck and upper chest were red with blood and he was bleeding worse than a stuck pig but he was still very much alive. Hatred animating his dark eyes, he hoisted Fargo half into the air and the fingers on Fargo's throat became a vise. "Die!" Toad roared, froth bubbling from his lips.

Fargo pressed the Remington muzzle against Toad's sloping forehead, thumbed back the hammer, and squeezed. At the blast Toad's head snapped back, his eyes rolled up in their sockets, and his prodigious strength fled his limbs. The grip on Fargo's throat relaxed. Pulling loose, Fargo pushed to his feet.

Hooves drummed. Amos Spack was escaping. Low over the saddle, he glanced back and glowered.

Fargo took aim but again hands closed on him, this time on his leg, and he was nearly upended. Charlie Grub had produced a dagger, which he sheared at Fargo's belly. Throwing himself to the left, Fargo sought to avoid the blow but he was only partially successful. The double-edged blade sliced through his skin and dug a furrow across his lower ribs. Not deep, but deep enough to cause him to wince.

"You bastard!" Grub raged. "You stinkin' bastard!"

Fargo leveled the Remington but Grub's other hand closed on the barrel and pushed. Simultaneously, he struck with the dagger.

Jerking his neck out of harm's way, Fargo grabbed

Grub's wrist and tried to tear the Remington loose but Grub clung on. Grub was fighting with the fierce desperation of the doomed, his features contorted in feral focus on the one thing that mattered to him— killing Fargo before he, himself, died.

A knee arced at Fargo's groin. Fargo shifted but pain exploded below his belt and it was all he could do to keep from letting go of Grub's wrist and doubling over, which would have proven fatal.

"You shot me!" Grub raged, as if it were unthinkable that someone would do such a thing to a cold-hearted killer who went around chopping prospectors into bits and pieces. "You shot me!"

Fargo dearly desired to shoot him again but Grub clung to the Remington's barrel with near-superhuman vitality. Then something swished through the air and a rifle stock connected with Grub's head. Grub sagged but he did not let go.

Maxine raised the rifle. She was a red-haired angel of vengeance with smoldering pits for eyes. "Damn you to hell!" She swung again. The sound of the hardwood stock slamming against Grub's ear was like the sound an axe made when it bit into the trunk of a pine tree.

Charlie Grub gasped and oozed to the dirt, blood staining his shirt and trickling from the new gash.

Jumping up, Fargo snatched the rifle from Maxine and whirled. Amos Spack was still within range. Fargo jammed the stock to his shoulder and fixed a bead but the next moment Spack vanished. It was as if the earth yawned wide and swallowed both the horse and its rider, which, Fargo, suspected, wasn't far from the truth. There must be a wash or gully Spack had reined into.

Fargo stood still, waiting, hoping against hope Spack would reappear. Seconds crawled by. Reluctantly, he lowered the rifle. "Damn the luck," he fumed.

"We're alive," Maxine said. Her gaze was riveted

on Toad and a scarlet pool forming under him. "Which is more than we can say about him."

"Would you rather it was me lying there?" Fargo gave the rifle to her and reclaimed his own guns. The Colt had blood on it, which he wiped off on Toad's pants.

"I never hit anyone like that," Maxine said. "God help me, but I wanted to kill him."

"They would have killed you," Fargo said to lessen her guilt. A groan reminded him Charlie Grub was still alive. He fed a round into the Henry's chamber. "One down, two to go."

"What are you fixing to do?" Maxine asked. "He can't hurt us. We should take him to town."

Charlie Grub picked that moment to stir. Groaning, he rose onto his elbows. He had been shot and clubbed but he was still breathing, and still dangerous.

"Lie still and we'll see what we can do to help you," Maxine told him.

Growling deep in his throat, Grub firmed his hold on his dagger and lunged, stabbing at her legs.

Fargo fired the Henry and Grub flopped onto his back. "And you wanted to help him," Fargo said to Maxine. He fired again and Grub convulsed and arched his back. A third shot caused Grub to go limp and expire with a loud exhale.

"He was trying to kill me," Maxine said in a mild daze. "Even after I offered to help him."

"What did you expect?" Fargo gruffly demanded. "They only kept you alive because Spack knew it gave him an edge over me." He glanced at her son. "How are you holding up?"

Donny Walters was trembling like an aspen leaf in a strong wind. He was as pale as paper and could not take his eyes off the bodies. "I never saw anyone killed before. It's scary."

"Sometimes a man isn't left any choice," Fargo said.

"You do it and put it behind you and don't think about it anymore."

"What about Spack?" Donny asked.

"What about him?"

"He won't give up, will he? Now that you've shot his friends, he'll want you dead more than ever."

"A lot of people have wanted me dead." Fargo walked past them to the other end of the clearing and the crumpled body next to the pine. In death Elias seemed to be smiling, as if the condition agreed with him. "Damn," Fargo said softly. Bending, he picked his friend up and carried him to a spot a dozen yards away. Since he didn't have a shovel, a broken limb had to suffice. Propping the Henry against a bole, he began digging.

"What are you doing?" Maxine and Donny had come over and were watching him.

"What does it look like?" Fargo snapped.

"I'm sorry," Maxine said. "I don't know what it is I've done but whatever it is, I'm truly and honestly sorry."

Fargo lanced the broken limb into the earth and flipped over a large clod. He shouldn't blame them for behaving as they were. Violent death was a shock to those unaccustomed to it. "You haven't done anything."

"Then why are you so mad?" Maxine asked.

Fargo touched Elias Dover with the branch. "This man was a friend of mine and I don't have a lot of friends to spare." He did not add that he felt partly to blame. He should never have let Elias tag along. Because he liked the old man, the old man was dead.

"Oh," Maxine said, and her features softened. "I'm sorry for your loss. I don't have a lot of good friends, either."

Fargo did not want them watching him. "Go gather up all the weapons you can find. We'll take them with us when we go."

Maxine did not move. Instead she said quietly, "Thank you for saving our lives. If not for you, we would be like your friend."

"Spack still might finish the job if we're not careful," Fargo said. And it would not do to forget they were in the heart of Apache country.

"Come, Donny," Maxine said. She took a few steps, then paused. "It must be hard being you," was her parting comment.

Fargo dug with renewed anger. It took half an hour to make a hole big enough, and even then it was not as deep as it needed to be to thwart scavengers so he dug down another foot. He was about to roll the body into the grave when he remembered to go through Elias' pockets. In one he found the paltry few dollars the old scout had left to his name, along with a small folding knife. In another he found a letter. It was from a Beverly Dover who lived in Philadelphia. He unfolded the letter and began to read it.

Grandfather. It was a joy hearing from you after so many months. I am sorry to hear about your eyes and the army letting you go. We all love you dearly but I must say no to your request. We simply do not have the room to take you in. As much as it would please me for you to live with us and listen to your tales of life—

Fargo stopped reading. He folded the letter and placed it back in Dover's pocket. "I really was your last hope," he said to the body, then rolled it into the hole and commenced covering it. He was mad, furious mad, and he did the job in half the time it would have taken if he were not. When at length he stood and brushed off his hands, Maxine and Donny were hunkered nearby.

"Why do things like this happen?" Maxine asked forlornly.

"You're asking me?" Fargo put a hand on her shoulder. "You need to be strong. You have your boy to think of."

"I'm trying," Maxine said. "I really am. But those awful men and what they said and did. I never thought something like this would happen to me."

"No one ever does." Fargo went to the horses. He brought back a mare and the pony. "I take it these are yours?"

"I wish they were," Maxine said. "Spack got them for us. Where, I couldn't say." She slowly rose, pulling Donny with her.

"They're yours now," Fargo said. He gave her a boost into the saddle and turned to help the boy but Donny had already forked leather.

"I'll never be the same after this," Maxine lamented. "As long as I live this day will affect everything I do."

Fargo stepped over to his own horse. "Only if you let it." He rigged a lead rope for the extra horses, climbed on the Ovaro, and lifted the reins.

"Wait," Maxine said, and nodded at Grub and Toad. "What about them?"

"Coyotes and buzzards have to eat, too." Fargo clucked to the Ovaro and headed west.

"Shouldn't we bury them?" Maxine persisted. "It's the Christian thing to do."

"If you want to that much, go right ahead," Fargo said. "But don't expect me to help and don't expect me to stay." He did not look back to see what she did and soon heard the clomp of hooves.

"Life isn't as it should be," Maxine said to his back.

"Whatever is?" was Fargo's rebuttal. He squared his shoulders and put Elias and Toad and Charlie Grub from his mind. "The important thing is that you and your son are alive."

"I'm sorry for being so addled."

"Quit apologizing," Fargo said. "Once was enough."

He rose in the stirrups to scan the countryside but nothing moved, not so much as an insect or a lizard. "We're not out of the woods yet."

"Amos Spack?" Maxine said.

"Among other things." Fargo brought the Ovaro to a canter and rode over a mile before he slowed. No puff of dust rose behind them or to either side. The three of them, and the horses, appeared to be the only living beings in the mountains. But Fargo wasn't fooled.

A high ridge appeared. It was quite a climb but once they reached the crest Fargo was treated to a panoramic view of the countryside. No one was following them. He went down the far slope and into a canyon and wound along it to a small valley where the vegetation was sparse and brown save for a patch of green on the other side. By then the sun was high in the sky.

Donny brought the pony alongside the Ovaro. "I want to be like you when I grow up, Mr. Fargo."

"Go back East," Fargo said. "You'll be happier." He made for the greenery.

"I could be happy being a scout and killing people when I had to," Donny responded. "You do it and you seem happy enough."

"Out here"—Fargo encompassed the valley and the mountains with a gesture—"a man does what he has to do. I only kill when I have to."

"My mother always said all killing is bad but how can it be bad to kill someone who is trying to kill you?" Donny asked.

"You can't go by what I do." Fargo remembered another young man who had looked up to him. He had not liked it then and he did not like it now. Fortunately, they came to the stand of trees, and as he suspected, within lay a spring. Not a big spring or a deep spring but enough water for the trees, and for them and their horses. "We'll stay here tonight."

Maxine squinted skyward. "It's early yet. Why stop so soon?"

"It's as good a place as any," Fargo hedged. The real reason might upset her. He stripped the horses and picketed them, then got a small fire going. By then Donny was curled up on a blanket, napping.

Maxine was stifling yawn after yawn. "Neither of us had much sleep last night. I tried but I was too worried." She tenderly placed a hand on her son's head. "If I lost him, life wouldn't be worth living."

"You should nap too," Fargo suggested. Snatching up the Henry, he moved toward the trees. "I'm going to stretch my legs." He was lying but it was best she did not know the truth.

"Be careful."

Once he was out of sight, Fargo crouched and glided from bole to bole until he was near the tall grass. He chose a suitable cottonwood and shimmied up it. The branches were thin. Only a few of the thickest could bear his weight. He chose the lowest on the off side.

The valley was empty of life save for a solitary doe grazing to the south. A young doe who did not know any better than to wander into the open. He would have liked to shoot it so they had fresh meat for supper but shots would carry a long way.

Fargo estimated sunset to be a couple of hours off yet.

When fishing it was always best to give the fish plenty of line. That applied to two-legged fish as well. So Fargo sat as still as granite and prayed Amos Spack would take the bait. He wasn't proud of what he was doing. The important thing was to end it. He could not spend the rest of his days looking over his shoulder.

Over half an hour went by. The doe drifted into the high grass, perhaps to bed down until the cool of evening, and the valley was undisturbed by other signs of life.

Fargo was so intent on the grass and the bordering

slopes that when he happened to glance down and beheld Maxine looking up at him with her hands on her hips, he was taken aback. He had not heard her come up. "I thought you were sleeping."

"What are you doing up there?" Maxine asked.

"Keeping watch," Fargo said, which was true as far as it went but there was more to it and she was no fool.

"I wondered why you stopped so early," Maxine said. "You're using us as bait, aren't you? You're hoping Spack comes after us so you can put a bullet in his brain."

Fargo did not answer because no answer was necessary.

"The least you could have done was told me. Donny and I should have a say. It's our lives at risk."

"I didn't want to worry you," Fargo said, which sounded as preposterous as it was.

Maxine shook her head. "You didn't want me saying no. You were afraid I would insist you take Donny and me on to Gila Bend." She paused. "I never imagined you could be so heartless."

Fargo fidgeted under her accusing gaze. "That's a strong word, don't you think?"

"Not strong enough. My son and I aren't sheep to be staked out to lure in a rabid wolf. We're human beings, damn it."

"I don't blame you for being mad."

"It's nice to have your approval," Maxine said scathingly, "but that's like closing the stable doors after the horses have got out. Honestly, I expected better of you after I've shared so much of myself."

"We can head out now if you want," Fargo offered. He did not want to but he would for her sake.

Maxine was a while answering. "No. It would be just as easy for him to pick us off out there."

"Easier." Fargo gripped a limb, carefully lowered himself until his legs were straight, and dropped the final six feet, tucking at the knees as he landed. "But it looks like he's not coming before dark."

"What makes you think he'll come at all? Wouldn't it be smarter for him to head for parts unknown?"

"It's personal for him now. Spack could never look at himself in the mirror ever again if he tucked his tail between his legs and lit a shuck. That, and for other reasons." Fargo did not elaborate.

Once again Maxine wasn't fooled. "For me, you mean? Avenge his friends and give in to his lust all at the same time?" She stared forlornly out across the mountains. "It's an ugly world we live in. I never realized how ugly until my husband went off and left me. And now this."

"Not all of it is ugly," Fargo said. Gently cupping her chin, he kissed her lightly on the lips. "Or have you forgotten?"

Maxine's grin was brazen. "How can I forget the most pleasurable night of my life?" She kissed him, only her kiss lasted longer. "What is it about you that makes me tingle so much? I'm all for doing it again if you're at all willing."

Fargo was more than happy to oblige her but he had Spack to think of. "Maybe later, once we're sure he's not coming." Better yet, after they reached town and had four walls around them.

"But later is when he is most liable to show up," Maxine said. "If I were him, I would wait until it's dark and slip in and slit our throats when you're not looking."

"Thanks for the confidence," Fargo said wryly, and turned. "You'd better go check on your son."

Maxine placed a hand on his arm and stepped up close to him, so close that her warm breath fluttered on his neck and the warmth of her body seemed to melt his buckskins from his. "We'll never have a better time."

Their eyes met. "Only when Spack is maggot food,"

Fargo refused to give in. "We're not eighteen years old."

"Spack won't come until nightfall. I'm sure of it. And Donny is so tired, he'll sleep for hours yet." Maxine ran a finger along his chin. "We don't have to take as long as last time."

"We shouldn't," Fargo said.

"Which is not the same as saying we can't." Maxine pressed against him. "What do you say?"

"I say you're crazier than the Renegade."

Maxine laughed throatily and looped her arms around his neck. "I'll take that as a yes."

11

Fargo never claimed to understand women. They could be irritatingly logical one minute and bafflingly illogical the next. It would never occur to him to want to make love while being stalked by a vicious killer.

"Is something wrong?" Maxine asked when he hesitated.

Fargo glanced into the stand and then at the south end of the valley and then at the north end. "No," he said, and almost laughed. Wrapping his free arm around her slender waist, he guided her a dozen steps to where three trees stood close together. Slipping between them, he pulled her in after him.

"Here?" Maxine said skeptically. "How on earth are we supposed to do it? There's not enough room to lie down."

"Who said anything about lying down?" Fargo leaned the Henry against the tree behind him, then pressed Maxine against the tree behind her. He cupped her bottom and squeezed, hard, and she gasped.

"Oh my. And here I thought you weren't interested." A sly smile curled her luscious lips.

Another thing Fargo would never savvy was why

women liked to pretend so much. Maxine wasn't fooling anyone. He wanted her and she knew it and she knew he knew she knew.

"We can't make a lot of noise, though," Maxine warned. "If Donny were to see us, I would be mortified."

"You're not the only one," Fargo said, eliciting a grin.

"Liar. It takes a lot to embarrass you, I suspect. When was the last time you were so flustered you turned beet red?"

Fargo thought that a damned silly question under the circumstances but he made a show of trying to remember, then shrugged.

"I was right." Maxine gave a toss of her head and her lustrous red hair cascaded over her shoulders. "So. See anything you like, handsome?"

"Lips that won't stop flapping when they should be doing this," Fargo said, and fused his mouth to hers. He did not close his eyes as he normally would, but glanced toward the spring, then to the north and to the south.

Maxine cooed softly. Her lips were as smooth as silk and as soft as a prime beaver pelt. Her tongue explored his lower teeth and then his upper, then met his in a velveteen waltz. Her hands stimulated him where he most liked being stimulated.

"What's this down here?" Maxine teased when they parted so she could catch her breath. "Do you always go around with a broom in your pants?"

Fargo glanced toward the spring and then at the north end of the valley and then the south end.

"Is something the matter? You seem a bit distracted."

"Think so?" Fargo said, and kissed her again while sculpting the soft contours of her backside as if her cheeks were clay and he was a master sculptor. She playfully ground her nether mound against his broom. He was so hard, he felt like his manhood would burst.

"Mmmmm," Maxine breathed when she drew her head from his. "You are the best kisser that ever lived."

"You're not bad yourself," Fargo complimented her, and stopped her from prattling on by molding their mouths together, and this time their bodies, as well. He roved his right hand from her buttocks around her hip to her belly and up to her left breast. Her nipple was like a tack. He pinched it through her dress and she squirmed and sought to inhale his tongue.

"The things you do to me," Maxine husked after a while. "You excite me like no man ever has."

Fargo kissed her ear and nibbled the lobe, then licked her neck and her throat and raised his mouth to hers. She kissed him hungrily, her bosom rising and falling faster than a few minutes ago. He sucked on her tongue and she sucked on his. He covered her other breast and pinched the nipple as he had the first and she thrust her hips against his in wanton invitation.

Fargo was warm all over, and growing warmer. He glanced toward the spring but not north and south, then slowly hiked at her dress until he had it up around her hips. He plunged a hand between them and stroked her through the chemise and her drawers and she shivered as if she were cold when actually she felt as warm as he was, if not warmer.

"Oh! Oh!" Maxine exclaimed when he touched her secret spot. "There! Right there!"

Fargo flicked her knob a few more times and each provoked a gasp and a quiver. He lathered her throat but did not undo the top of her dress. They had to use a little common sense whether she wanted to or not.

Then Maxine boldly placed her hands on his pole

and lightly stroked it. Fargo thought he would erupt then and there. His throat constricted and the trees seemed to spin and he had to blink to clear his vision so he could glance toward the spring.

"You like that, don't you?" Maxine taunted.

"I like this, too," Fargo said. Without her being aware, he had parted her underthings. Now, in one quick motion, he inserted his finger between her nether lips, delving as deep as it would go.

"Ahhhhh!" Arching her back, Maxine uttered a long sigh, then languidly smiled. "Keep that up, if you please."

Fargo intended to. He slid his finger almost out and then in again. She was wet for him, her inner walls an exquisite sheath awaiting his sword.

"It's too bad—" Maxine began, but she did not say what was too bad and Fargo did not ask. She kissed him. Her fingernails dug into his shoulders. If not for his buckskin shirt, she would have drawn blood.

Fargo added a second finger to the first. Her forehead touched his and she clung to him, wearing her need on her sleeve, as it were. He pumped his fingers and her walls closed around them.

"Yesssssssss. Oh, yesssssssss."

Once again Fargo glanced all around. The trees were quiet and the valley was still. Reaching down, he started to undo his buckle but she pushed his hand away and undid it herself. Then she pried at his pants until the only thing keeping them up was his engorged manhood.

Maxine stared at it and licked her lips. "Now," she requested. "He could wake up at any time."

Gripping her hips, Fargo aligned himself with her slit and lightly ran the tip of his member back and forth. She quaked with rising need and tried to impale herself but he drew away and grinned.

"You're positively awful," Maxine said.

"I've been called worse." Fargo rammed up into her and she nearly came off the ground. Her mouth opened as if she were going to scream but all that issued from her throat was the lowest of moans. He stood still and she stood still, and he could feel his heart hammer in his chest.

Maxine rested her chin on his chest. "Make me forget. Let there just be you and me and nothing else."

That was easily accomplished. Fargo levered up onto the balls of his feet, nearly lifting her off her feet. Maxine's legs rose and hooked around his waist and she gripped his shoulders and looked him in the eyes.

"It won't take much."

It didn't. At Fargo's fourth stroke she cried out, softly, and her bottom went into a frenzy of motion, rising and falling with the impassioned fever of a rhythm as old as the human race.

Fargo controlled himself but it was not easy. He rode out her release, and when she was done, when she had gushed not once but several times and collapsed against him, spent, he stroked harder and faster.

Maxine's head came up. Her red hair was plastered to her face and her lips were as full as the fullest of strawberries. Her beautiful eyes widened slightly, and she said simply, "Oh God."

Fargo concentrated on not exploding before he was ready. He rocked and rocked, thrusting his pole deep up into her, more times then he could care to count, and each time a satiny ripple of pleasure ran from the base of his spine to the nape of his neck and his whole body tingled. There was no holding back. He held her close and rammed into her and she took him, took all of him, and bliss coursed through him, the only true bliss there was. He could never get enough of it.

Afterward, Fargo coasted to a stop and they stood

chest to breasts, gulping air and covered with sweat and not caring. Maxine's fingers tiredly rose to his hair and she whispered in his ear, "You're magnificent."

Fargo could say the same of her but he did not say anything. He opened his eyes and glanced toward the spring and at the north end of the valley and then at the south end of the valley. He sighed in relief as much as contentment.

"I wish I had met you before I met my husband," Maxine commented.

It was a sign. Fargo slowly pulled out of her and did up his pants and strapped on his gun belt.

Maxine smoothed out her skirt as best she could. Finishing, she leaned back against the tree, her dress as rumpled as her hair, her eyes gleaming with the inner light of complete contentment. "If you ever tire of wandering, look me up."

"By then you'll have another husband," Fargo predicted. She liked it too much to go without, and she had her son.

"I would wait for—" Maxine started to say.

"Don't." Fargo placed a finger to her lips. "Don't spoil it. When this is over we'll go our own ways and that will be that."

"I know," Maxine said unhappily. "You were honest with me from the beginning. But a girl can always hope, can't she?"

The question did not merit an answer. Fargo lowered the hem of her dress to where it should be and smoothed it. "Next time find a man who isn't a jackass."

Maxine traced the outline of his right ear with her fingernail. "What a nice thing to say." She straightened and fiddled with her hair. "I could use a brush or a comb."

"I have a comb in my saddlebags," Fargo offered. She clasped his hand and they strolled toward the spring like two lovers. He held the Henry close to his right leg with his thumb on the hammer.

"I saw you watching everything. You think Spack will show up before nightfall, don't you?"

"It could be any time," Fargo said.

"What's to stop him from lying out in the grass and shooting us from far off?" Maxine brought up. "It's the safe thing for him to do."

"He'll want to rub my nose in it," Fargo said. "He'll want to be up close so he can see my eyes when he does it." He paused. "It's what I would do."

"But he's not you. I suspect he's a coward at heart. He rode off and left his friends, didn't he?"

"He didn't want to die," Fargo said. "That wasn't yellow, that was smart."

"You give him too much credit," Maxine disagreed. "Killers aren't smart or they wouldn't be killers."

"You've muddied the waters," Fargo told her.

"But don't you see? A killer isn't a normal person like you and me. Anyone who can murder another living person has something wrong with them. Something terribly wrong. They don't think like you and I do."

"I've killed. Outlaws kill. Apaches kill whites, Apaches kill Mexicans. The Sioux kill anyone they catch in their territory." Fargo could go on but didn't.

"That's different," Maxine said. "You kill because you have to. Spack kills to fill his pockets. Don't you see?"

Fargo saw, if she didn't. They emerged from the trees and he saw the blanket and stopped dead.

Maxine noticed his expression, and looked, and the gasp torn from her was a gasp of total terror. "Donny! Where is he?"

The blanket the boy had been sleeping on was empty. The camp was undisturbed, the fire crackling softly, the horses dozing.

"Maybe he's looking for us," Fargo said.

Maxine let go of his hand and moved to the spring. "Donny!" she hollered. "Where are you?"

137

The silence prickled the short hairs on Fargo's neck. If his carelessness cost the boy his life, he would never forgive himself. He walked past the spring to a thicket and rose onto his toes to scour the vegetation.

"Where can he be?" Maxine's anxiety was mounting. "He has to be around here somewhere."

Just then the brush rustled and opened and out came Donny. Tears moistened his face and fear filled his eyes, with good reason. Behind him, a hand clamped to the back of his neck, came his captor, holding a knife pressed to Donny's jugular.

"Dear God!" Maxine blurted. "Who are you? Why are you doing this?"

The man tittered, and the titter was not quite sane. Bedraggled brown hair hung past his shoulders. He was white but his skin had been bronzed by the sun to where he could pass for an Apache. A tattered, grimy shirt hung from his scarecrow frame. His pants were in worse shape. His clothes were a white man's clothes but not his footwear. He wore Apache moccasins. Old moccasins that rose almost to his knees over his pants. He had a beard, another white trait, and a headband like the Apaches wore. As remarkable as his clothes were, his eyes were more so. A vivid green, they held a gleam that explained the titter.

"Meet the Renegade," Fargo said. He was tempted to whip his Henry up and fire but if the first shot was not a killing shot, Donny Walters would pay with his life.

The man tittered again, louder than before, and bobbed his chin. "Lose the rifle and the revolver, if you please, and even if you don't."

"He speaks English," Maxine said.

"Why wouldn't he?" Fargo responded while carefully lowering the Henry. The truth had suddenly hit him. "Meet Desmond Hammond."

The Renegade blinked and tilted his head and his insane eyes gleamed more brightly. "Do I know you?"

"Your daughter Clarice hired me to find you." Fargo placed his arms at his sides, hoping Hammond would forget about the Colt.

"Clarice?" the Renegade said, his brow knitting. "I seem to remember someone by that name."

"You have another daughter named Millicent and a son called Frank and another called Dexter," Fargo prodded. "And a wife, Janet."

Desmond Hammond recoiled. All the blood drained from him, and his eyes grew wilder than ever. "Her! The bitch! She's the one! She's the one who made me what I am!"

"Your wife?" Maxine said. "I don't understand." She took a step toward them but froze when the Renegade suddenly gouged the tip of the blade into her son's neck, drawing a drop of blood.

"Hold it! No closer, either of you, or the boy dies!" Hammond twisted the knife slightly, and Donny cringed. "Don't think I won't! I've done it many a time!"

"We know," Fargo said, forcing himself to remain calm. "But we don't know why."

"It was her." Hammond's jaw muscles twitched, his right eyelid drooped half shut, and spittle dribbled over his lower lip. It happened so abruptly, it was startling. His voice rising, he nearly screeched, "Her nagging and her bossing and always telling me what to do and how to think! I hate her! Hate her, hate her, hate her!" He started shaking, and the knife came dangerously close to Donny's jugular.

Fargo was about to draw his Colt and risk a shot when Maxine hurled herself at Hammond.

"Don't!" she wailed. "He's my son!"

The Renegade gripped the boy's hair and bent Donny's head back to better expose his throat. Instantly, Maxine halted.

"Please! I'm begging you! He's all I have in this world!"

"You think I care?" Hammond snarled. His whole face was twitching now and his eyes were maniacal pits. They focused on Fargo. "Are your ears plugged? I told you to drop the damn revolver and I meant it!"

Fargo was sure he could put a slug into Hammond's head before Hammond cut Donny's throat but the madman was cleverer than he gave him credit for being. Suddenly Hammond ducked behind Donny so only his arm and the knife were visible.

"Last chance! I'll count to ten." The Renegade cackled. "One. Three. Six. Eight."

By then Fargo had the Colt in his hand and was slowly placing it next to the Henry. It galled him. He supposed he should be grateful Hammond hadn't slain them or the boy outright, but a quick death beat a slow, agonizing death any day. "There. It's down. Now we can talk."

"Talk?" Desmond Hammond shoved Donny at Maxine. A pistol blossomed in his left hand, trained on Fargo. "I let my knife do my talking these days. An ear here, a nose there. And don't forget the tongues. I do so love to cut out the tongues."

Maxine held Donny protectively to her. "I don't get any of this. How can you be the Renegade? The Renegade is supposed to be an Apache."

Hammond cackled and slapped his thigh. "That's what they think, is it? Mostly I kill them before they can talk, but you being a woman and all, I can make an exception." He stopped and began shaking anew. "That other one is a woman, too! A devil woman. The bitch of bitches."

"Who is he talking about?"

"His wife, Janet," Fargo said.

Desmond Hammond took a step back, his right eyelid drooping further, and words spilled from him in a rush. "You've met her? Then you know. She's evil! As heartless as can be! All those years. The constant carping. Do this! Do that! Her way or no way. Never once could I please her. Never once did I do anything right." His whole body was twitching and spittle oozed from the corners of his mouth.

"Dear God in heaven," Maxine breathed.

Hammond spun on her like a striking rattler. "God? What the hell does God have to do with anything? As if there is one!" He muttered something, then said, "Would God have let her do that to me?"

"Do what?" Maxine asked.

Fargo tried to catch her attention so he could warn her. Desmond Hammond was a deranged keg of black powder fit to explode if they were not careful.

"Grind me under her heel, she did! I tried and tried but I couldn't make her happy. I always fell short. Nothing I ever did pleased her. Not once our entire marriage. I'm not a man, she said, only a mockery pretending to be a man! So she never let me do anything on my own."

"Until you couldn't take it anymore," Fargo said when Hammond stopped. "You wanted to prove her wrong. You wanted to show her you could do something right. That you were a man, after all. So you came here looking for silver."

Hammond absently nodded. "How was I to know how hard it would be? I searched and searched but everyone was finding ore except me. They laughed at me, the other prospectors. Called me useless, just like she always did. I was so mad, you wouldn't believe. Then one night I came on an old Apache high up in the mountains. He was just sitting there, looking sort of sickly, and singing to himself. It was the strangest thing. I tried to sneak away but he saw me. I was afraid he would call others so I ran up and stabbed him, and just like that he died." Hammond stopped. "I never knew killing was so easy."

Fargo hoped they could keep him talking. He edged his right foot forward and then his left.

"I can't describe what it did to me," Hammond had

141

gone on. "I felt different, somehow. I felt good. I sat there and cut the old Apache's heart from his chest and I ate it like my grandfather used to eat raw buck hearts."

"Sweet Jesus!" Maxine exclaimed.

"It's not like you think. It's wonderful. It's invigorating. It's"—Hammond seemed to search for the right word—"it's a tonic for the soul. For the first time in my life I saw everything so clearly. I saw what I had let her make of me and what I had to do to those who had laughed at me."

"To the other prospectors?" Maxine said.

"Always pointing at me and whispering. Always mocking me. Saying I didn't know what I was doing and I would never strike it rich. They sounded just like her. Although she was worse. Much, much worse."

Fargo tried to imagine what it must have been like. For over twenty years Hammond let his wife belittle him and boss him around and treat him as if he were worthless. All Desmond Hammond ever wanted was to be a man. But things were not as he expected and Hammond failed at prospecting as he had failed at life. His wife would never let him hear the end of it.

Then came the night Hammond stumbled on an old Apache singing his death chant, and slew him. Desmond Hammond discovered there was one thing he could do, and do well, a thing many men could not bring themselves to do because they did not have it in them—to kill without regard.

Fargo suddenly realized Hammond was addressing him.

"How did you know? The moment you saw me, you knew I was the Renegade. Was it the moccasins?"

"The tracks you left," Fargo said. "White men and Apaches don't walk the same. White man walk with their toes pointed out and take long steps. Apaches walk more on the balls of their feet and take shorter steps. The first time I saw the Renegade's tracks I knew the Renegade was a white man."

"Perceptive of you," Hammond said.

"Not really," Fargo said. "For a while I was sure a man named Spack was the Renegade and you were dead." He edged his left foot forward a few inches.

For a minute there, Hammond had stopped twitching and seemed perfectly sane. But now his eyelid drooped and his face contorted and he pointed the revolver at Fargo's belly. "Enough jabbering. I'll do you first, then the woman, then the boy."

12

There was the loud blast of a shot. Involuntarily, Fargo flinched. Maxine screamed his name and even Donny yelped in fright. But there was no piercing impact of a slug. Fargo did not feel anything because he was not the one who had been shot.

Desmond Hammond melted to the earth with a bewildered expression on his face. Belatedly, he clutched at his head, or tried to, and then was covered with blood seeping from his scalp.

Fargo spun toward the Henry and the Colt but he was a shade too slow.

"Take another step and you die that much sooner," Amos Spack warned as he emerged from the trees with his smoking rifle in his hands. "Not that I would mind shootin' you where you stand but I have a better way in mind."

Maxine was stunned by the turn of events, and gasped in disbelief.

"What's the matter, red?" Spack baited her. "Thought you'd seen the last of me? Not likely, when I owe this bastard for buckin' my pards out in gore." Spack stopped and looked from her to Fargo to Desmond Hammond. "So this was the Renegade? I'd never have suspected."

"What do you plan to do with us?" Maxine found her voice.

Spack laughed coldly and said to Fargo, "Ever notice how females ask the dumbest questions? Why don't you tell her since I'm sure a smart hombre like you has it all figured out."

"You'll take Hammond to Gila Bend and claim the reward," Fargo said. "A thousand dollars is too much to pass up."

"Damn right it is," Spack said. "With that and Toad's and Grub's share of our takin's, I'll have enough for San Francisco."

"As for the three of us, we know too much for him to let us live."

"See?" Spack grinned. "You *are* a bright one. The only thing you left out was how I aim to kill you."

"Aren't you going to shoot us?" Maxine asked.

"And spoil my fun?" Spack's grin widened. "Besides, if I shoot you, no one will blame the Renegade."

Maxine put a hand to her throat. "You wouldn't."

"Hell, yes, I would," Spack said. "I'll carve up your boyfriend so it looks like the Renegade did it. Then you and me will do what you and him were doing over in the trees a while ago."

"You saw us?" Maxine could barely get the words out.

"Not as much as I would have liked," Spack said. "I was too far off in the grass. But I could tell you were havin' a grand old time."

Donny broke his silence with, "What is he talking about, Ma?"

"Nothing, son," Maxine said, but she was a vivid shade of red and she averted her gaze from Amos Spack.

"This couldn't have turned out better if I'd planned

it," the killer remarked, "and just when I reckoned everything was against me." He nudged Hammond's body with his boot. "If this yack were still alive I'd thank him for solving all my problems."

"You're not the only one with a grudge to settle," Fargo bid for time. "You have my friend's death to answer for."

"The difference is that I hold all the high cards." Spack stepped past Hammond so he was close to them. "Let's get this over with. I want you on your knees with your hands behind your back so your lady friend here can tie you up."

"Never!" Maxine snapped. "Once I do, we're at your mercy. Nothing you can say or do will make me."

"Oh?" Spack swivelled and trained his rifle on Donny. "Does the brat mean that little to you? Because if you don't go to those horses and get a rope and truss him up good and proper, your son dies before either of you."

Donny grasped his mother's arm. "I'm not afraid, Ma. Don't you do it."

Suddenly Fargo noticed something none of the others saw. He had to keep Spack talking awhile, and maybe, just maybe, they would live to see the sunset. "I've been to San Francisco a few times," he commented.

Spack's eyes narrowed. "Why in hell bring that up now?" But he was interested and he could not resist asking, "Is it all everyone says? A saloon on every corner and more willin' women than a man can shake a stick at?"

"The ladies wear nicer clothes than most places," Fargo said, "and they cost a lot more."

"But are they pretty?" Spack wanted to know. "A gambler told me all the fillies do up their hair and always smell nice and treat a gent like he's a king." A dreamy look came over him. "I'll be in heaven."

"Or hell," Fargo said, "and sooner than you think."

He saw Desmond Hammond's arm move as it had a minute ago. Not much, no more than an inch or so, enough to show he was alive. Hammond had dropped his knife but still had his pistol. His eyes opened and he stared blankly at the sky.

"You're threatenin' me?" Spack said, and chuckled. "For a man about to be carved into little pieces, you're mighty sure of yourself."

Hammond's head moved, and his eyelid drooped, and his face began to twitch.

"Practice much with that rifle of yours?" Fargo asked.

Spack quizzically cocked his head. "I take it back. You ask dumber questions than she does."

"A man needs to practice to keep his eye in," Fargo said.

"I know that," Spack said indignantly. "What do you take me for? And why bring it up?"

"I take you for someone who should have lit a shuck while he had the chance," Fargo replied, and smiled. "Your aim was off."

"My aim?" Spack repeated. It hit him, then, and he whirled, but Desmond Hammond had sat up and was holding the revolver at arm's length. Not steady, but steady enough, and at the crack of the shot Amos Spack was jolted onto his heels, blood bursting from his upper back.

Spack fired but missed. Staggering as if drunk, he bolted for the trees. Hammond thumbed back the hammer and squeezed the trigger and there was a *click*. A misfire. Then he was up, racing after Spack.

Fargo dived for the Henry and wedged the stock to his shoulder but they had both vanished into the vegetation. Maxine and Donny were riveted in shock, which was just as well since any movement might have drawn Hammond's attention. Snatching up his Colt, Fargo shoved it into its holster. "The horses!" he said, and had to give Maxine a shove to galvanize her to life.

Off in the trees a shot sounded and was answered by another.

Maxine helped her son onto the pony while Fargo covered them. She climbed on the mare, lifted the reins, and looked down. "What are you waiting for?"

"It has to end here," Fargo said. "Take all the other horses except mine with you."

"No. We'll stay and help."

"I can't watch my back and yours, both," Fargo said while handing her the other reins. "Do it for Donny if you won't do it for me."

Maxine balked, biting her lower lip. "But there are two of them and only one of you, and one of them is out of his mind."

Fargo did not have time for this. He slapped the pony on the flank and it trotted eastward. Left with no other recourse, Maxine slapped her long legs against the mare and hurried to catch up.

Crouching, Fargo ran to where the two men had entered the undergrowth. All was quiet again. He stalked forward, careful not to step on a twig. Spack and Hammond could not have gotten far. They might be anywhere in the stand, either stalking each other or maybe both had gone to ground and each was waiting for the other to blunder and give his presence away.

Stopping every few feet to look and listen, Fargo covered about thirty feet when the brush to his right shook as if from a strong wind, only there was no wind. Pivoting, he centered the Henry on the spot but no one appeared. The rustling stopped and the stand was quiet again.

The best scouts were some of the best hunters. They had to be. Not only did they guide boy soldiers barely old enough to shave through wild country the boy soldiers would become hopelessly lost in on their own, but a scout also had to find the food that kept the boy soldiers alive. A scout had to know the game that lived in any given part of the wilds, whether it be the mountains, the plains or the desert. He had to know where to find the game at any given hour of the day, and be able to stalk and kill however many animals were needed to fill the boy soldiers' bellies.

No trooper had ever gone hungry when Fargo was the scout. He could stalk and kill as silently and swiftly as an Apache. That included men, when he had to, and as fate would have it, he had to a lot.

Now, with a lunatic and a murderer to deal with, Fargo must rely on all the skill he possessed. Either of his enemies would kill him without batting an eye. One mistake, and it could be his last.

As motionless as a log, Fargo waited for a telltale flash of movement. But Spack had not lasted so long by being stupid, and Hammond had the feral instincts of the mindlessly insane to rely on.

Minutes crawled on leaden legs. Time seemed to stand still, as if the stand was aware of the tableau being played out and was holding its breath waiting for the outcome.

Fargo dismissed the silly notion and probed the trees. He must concentrate, must not let his thoughts wander.

A sparrow flew into sight, veered widely around a small pine, and arced higher into the sky.

His cheek to the Henry, Fargo glided toward the pine. The bird had acted as if something were there, something it was afraid of. He skirted the pine to the right, his finger curled around the trigger. The lowest branches were so low to the ground that a man might be under them.

A bead of sweat trickled down Fargo's forehead and into his right eye and he blinked to relieve the sting. He was almost past the pine. Every nerve tingling, he took a final step. Disappointment rippled through him. No one was there.

Lowering the Henry, Fargo was turning when he

149

saw the blood. Bright red splotches, freshly made. He remembered the shots he had heard. Cautiously advancing, he found a trail of splotches leading to the west. He found footprints, too. Moccasin tracks, more deeply impressed into the soil than they should be. There was only one explanation.

Fargo ran. He was almost to the end of the stand when hoofs drummed and he saw the rider in the distance, too far for a certain shot, a flopping form draped behind the saddle.

"Damn." Fargo sprinted for the spring. Without breaking stride he hurtled into the clearing and vaulted onto the Ovaro. He had faith his horse could overtake his quarry but the rider had a large lead. It would take a while.

For over half an hour Fargo rode westward. Then the tracks angled to the northwest and a particularly stark range few white men ever penetrated. Now and then he caught sight of a spot of blood but most of the bleeding had stopped.

At the bottom of a barren slope crowned by a boulder-strewn bluff, Fargo reined up. No sooner had he done so than a scream rose shrilly into the pale blue sky. A scream of torment and terror. A scream the likes of which human ears should never have to hear.

Dismounting, Fargo climbed on foot. It would not do to have the Ovaro take a stray bullet. Another scream echoed among the mountains, ending in a wavering gurgle. His body a coiled spring, he kept the Henry to his shoulder.

Near the summit Fargo heard a new sound, a low murmuring or babbling. He came to the boulders. Someone laughed, but not a normal laugh. It was the keening, brittle, fluttering mirth of total madness.

Fargo threaded in among the boulders. He swung to the left and stopped cold, his stomach churning.

Amos Spack was flat on his back. His ears and nose had been cut off, all three lined up in a neat row.

"Please," Spack said so softly that Fargo barely heard.

Desmond Hammond snickered. "That's it. Beg. I love it when they beg. Do it again while you still have your tongue." He wagged the blood-drenched knife in his right hand. "Let me hear you."

"End it," Spack begged.

"Not for a while yet," the Renegade said. "Not until you're flopping about like a goose with its head chopped off."

"Hammond," Fargo said.

The Renegade who was not really a renegade calmly glanced over a shoulder. "You! How did you find us? Go away. Can't you see I'm busy?"

"Put down the knife," Fargo said. "I'll take you to Gila Bend. Your daughters and sons are worried about you." He fixed the Henry's sights smack between Hammond's eyes. "Do you remember them? Do you remember my saying Clarice hired me to bring you back?"

Desmond Hammond touched the tip of his knife to his chin and scrunched up his face. "Why does that name sound so familiar? It's almost as if I should know who she is but I can't place her."

"She's your daughter." Fargo attempted to dispel the fog that had Hammond's mind in the grip of befuddlement. "She loves you and cares for you."

"I don't remember her, no," Hammond said. "Nor any sons, neither." His tone hardened. "All I remember is *her*. The bitch! The one who never let me be! The one who never let me stand on my own two feet." Tittering, Hammond nodded at his grisly handiwork. "Well, I'm standing on them now."

"Put down the knife," Fargo tried one last time.

"I've always wondered what it will be like, after,"

151

Hammond said. "I've always thought it will be the only real peace I'll know."

Fargo held the Henry perfectly steady.

"Why does my head hurt so much?" Hammond asked, and uncoiled with his revolver rising from his waist in a draw that was lightning fast.

The Henry thundered and Hammond flipped onto his back on top of Amos Spack. His arms waved wildly and his leg thrashed and then he went limp and the revolver fell to the dirt.

Fargo went over and dragged the body to one side. The horse had been left to wander and it took him a while to find it among the boulders and bring it back so he could tie Hammond's body behind the saddle. Then, the reins in hand, he headed for the bottom of the bluff.

A ragged whisper from Spack gave him pause. "What about me?"

"What about you?" Fargo noticed a trio of large ants crawling on one of the shredded ears.

"You can't leave me like this."

"Sure I can." Fargo took another stride.

"Wait!" Spack cried in terror, and broke into a fit of coughing that ended with drops of blood trickling from both sides of his mouth. "I could take a long time dyin'."

"There's that," Fargo said. More ants had joined.

"I'm askin' you, man to man." Spack would not give up.

"Go to hell."

The screams started when Fargo was halfway to the bottom. He mounted the Ovaro and rode eastward. For a long time he could hear them, growing weaker and weaker. Then they stopped and he brought the Ovaro to a trot.

It wasn't quite over. There was the mother and the boy, in the middle of Apache country. He rode hard for the stand thinking to pick up their trail but when he came to the spring, there they were. He climbed down and Maxine flew to him and flung her arms around his chest.

"You're alive! I was so worried!" She drew back and regarded the body. "What about Amos Spack?"

Fargo shook his head.

"I can't say I'm sorry," Maxine said. "If ever there was a man who deserved to die, it was him." She plucked at a whang on his sleeve. "Should we spend the night here and head back in the morning?"

"We start back now," Fargo informed her. Gunshots carried a long way. Any Apaches in the vicinity were bound to investigate.

Maxine looked disappointed. "Oh. I just thought—" She did not finish, and her cheeks colored pink.

By sunset they had covered a goodly number of miles. It was then Fargo shifted in the saddle and said to her, "I have a favor to ask."

"Anything," Maxine said, smiling warmly. "Anything at all."

"Desmond Hammond wasn't the Renegade."

Maxine and Donny both glanced at him and the boy blurted, "But he was! We knew he was!"

"Hush," Maxine said, studying Fargo as she had never studied him before. "Then who takes the blame, as if I can't guess?"

"Spack and Toad and Grub. They killed most of the prospectors anyway, so adding a few more to their tally won't change things much."

Donny still did not understand. "He wants us to lie, Ma. But you always said. lying is bad."

"It is," Maxine said. "This isn't the same. Desmond Hammond has two daughters and two sons."

"So?" Donny said.

Fargo spoke before Maxine. "So would you want to find out your mother was the Renegade?"

"That's silly," Donny said, and chuckled. Then he stared at the body, which Fargo had wrapped in a blanket before leaving the spring, and grew somber. "I think I get what you're saying. You want everyone to blame those other three so Mr. Hammond's sons and daughters won't feel bad."

"I won't do it if you don't agree," Fargo said. "Take your time making up your mind. We won't reach town for a few days yet."

"No need to take my time," the boy said. "If my ma says it's the right thing to do, then it's the right thing to do."

They were dusty and tired when they wound out of the mountains and along Gila Bend's main street to the general store. The closest thing to a mayor the town had was the owner of the general store, who listened avidly, then rushed out to spread the tidings.

Maxine and Donny were out on the boardwalk when Fargo emerged, Maxine swatting at her clothes. "Did he ask any questions?"

"Why should he?" Fargo rejoined, and casually remarked, "We'll split the reward. Use your half to move East like you've been wanting to."

For a few seconds Maxine was too stunned to say anything. "Five hundred dollars? I can't accept that much."

"Sure you can," Fargo touched her cheek. "If anyone has earned it, it's you." He nodded at the boy, and turned.

"Will I see you again?"

"It depends," Fargo said. He had one loose end to wrap up and then he would be on his way. With his half of the reward and the three hundred Clarice Hammond was paying him, he could afford a week of whiskey, women and cards in Santa Fe, or maybe Denver.

Fenton Wilson spotted Fargo the moment he entered the hotel. Wilson clapped him on the arms and beamed. "I just heard! Spack and his friends did all the killing! And you even found Hammond! You're everything folks say you are."

Fargo debated whether to do it there or somewhere less public and decided to hell with it. "I brought Maxine and Donny back safe and sound. She sure is some woman, that gal."

"I've always thought so," Fenton said.

Fargo stepped to the front window and scanned the street. He could see his reflection, among others. "Yes, sir. She's the kind of woman who can fill a single man's head with ideas about vows and altars."

"You don't say."

"But why buy the cow when you've had the milk for free?" Fargo asked, and did not receive an answer.

A buckboard clattered past the window. A grizzled prospector with a wad of tobacco bulging his cheek sauntered by chomping lustily.

"I sure did like running my fingers through her hair," Fargo went on, never taking his eyes off the reflections. "She reminds me of a dove I knew in San Antonio. Naked, they're enough alike to be twins." He paused. "Don't tell anyone, but she has a mole on her left thigh just above the knee."

An inarticulate growl filled the lobby. Fargo spun as Fenton Wilson sprang, a slim knife high in the hotel owner's right hand. Consumed by rage, Wilson stabbed at Fargo's throat but Fargo sidestepped, gripped Wilson's wrists, pivoted at the hip, and tossed him against a chair.

Both the chair and Wilson crashed to the floor. The knife went skittering. Wilson pushed to his hands and knees and looked up into the muzzle of Fargo's Colt. "You wouldn't!"

"Try me," Fargo said. "It was you who sicced Sam the cook on me. It's you who has been giving her gifts and trying to force her into marrying you even though she doesn't want to."

Wilson was livid. "She told you?"

"She's too much of a lady." Fargo let down the hammer and twirled the Colt into his holster. He waited for Wilson to stand, then drove his fist into the pit of Wilson's stomach. When the gasping and groaning and flopping ceased, and Wilson lay glaring up at him, he said, "I'll only say this once. Force yourself on her again, in any way, and you answer to me."

"After I treated you so kindly, too," Wilson spat through clenched teeth. "I thought you were special."

"You thought wrong." Fargo went out and saw Maxine and Donny walking east toward the boarding-house. The sway of her hips and the play of the sunlight on her hair stirred recent memories. "Another day or two won't matter," he said to himself, and hurried to catch up.

LOOKING FORWARD!
**The following is the opening
section of the next novel in the exciting
Trailsman series from Signet:**

THE TRAILSMAN #289

RENEGADE RAIDERS

*Indian Territory, 1859—
where the War of the Plains is
about to erupt, and, for Fargo,
all the omens point to death.*

Skye Fargo's idle thoughts were suddenly scattered
by a spine-tingling scream from the mounted column
behind him. The desperate trill raised the fine hairs
on the back of his neck. Only the worst agony in the
world could cause a cry like that.

His head swiveled around just in time to watch a
swollen-faced cavalry trooper slide out of his saddle

and land in a heap beside the dusty trail. The fallen man's body spasmed violently for a moment, then went limp in death.

"Dismount and take cover!" roared the young shavetail lieutenant in charge. "Hold your fire until you have confirmed targets!"

His men obeyed instantly, swinging down and leading their mounts into the screening timber. But neither the crop-bearded, buckskin-clad Fargo nor his fellow scout, a grizzled old explorer named Yellowstone Jack, bothered to take cover.

"This ain't the main attack," Jack said scornfully as they wheeled their mounts and rode back toward the dead man. "It's meant to get us in pursuit so's these red sons can ambush us when they choose."

Fargo nodded. "But there's still a few watching us now."

He was closely studying the cottonwood trees and thick patch of hawthorn bushes covering the slope to their right. The army unit had been following a timber-girt backwater of the river red men called *Akenzea,* and white men Arkansas. This spot was almost smack in the middle of The Nations—the vast Indian Territory, established not long after the War of 1812 as a permanent Indian home south of Kansas and immediately beyond the western borders of Missouri and Arkansas.

"There's one," Fargo said quietly, spotting an oval face painted green, yellow, and red. "A Kiowa intruder. I warned the kid to put flankers out."

"And the bone breastplate I spotted," Jack said, "was Staked Plain Comanches. Here to stir up the shit. Kiowas and Comanches . . . them two tribes don't never get together 'cept to kill and plunder."

By this time both riders, rifles to hand, had reached the fallen trooper. They could hear a few unshod ponies escaping toward the river and the scant-grown hills beyond. Fargo knew pursuing them was folly. A typical day's progress for a cavalry unit was about twenty-five miles; a fleeing Indian could cover as much as seventy.

"Hold in place, men!" the freckle-faced kid in charge of the soldiers shouted in a voice made reedy with nervousness. "They may mount a follow-on assault."

Fargo and Yellowstone Jack exchanged grins as they swung down. Jack was a head shorter than Fargo, but burly. He wore a slouched beaver hat and moccasins with hard soles of buffalo hide. His grizzled beard showed more salt than pepper.

" 'Follow-on assault.' " Jack sputtered with mirth. "Jimmy's a good lad, but he's fresh off ma's milk."

"No, he's fresh off the horseshit taught at West Point," Fargo said. "Takes a while to flush that rule book stuff out—"

Fargo suddenly fell silent as he got a better look at the dead soldier.

Yellowstone Jack, too, had just spotted what had riveted Fargo's attention. "Jesus Christ with a wooden leg!"

Both men knelt and stared at a gray-green face now swollen twice its normal size. A small, fletched dart protruded from his neck.

"Recognize that dart?" Fargo asked grimly, brass-framed Henry balanced across his thighs.

"You see any green on my antlers?" Jack demanded. He dug at a tick in his grizzled beard. "It's Cheraws."

He used the old mountain man name for Cherokees. No one knew for sure just what plant or plants provided the deadly poison used so effectively by Cherokees, but there was no denying they were experts with their long-rifled blowguns. The virulent poison was both agonizing and fast-acting.

"It makes me ireful, Skye, it truly does," Jack muttered. "That Cheraw pizen is a hard way to give up the ghost. Mebbe that army report Jimmy showed us is right, after all, 'bout a Cheraw uprising in The Nations."

Fargo's shrewd, sun-crinkled, lake-blue eyes gazed all around them speculatively.

"Your calves are gone to grass, you old fool," he said. "Sure, a renegade Cherokee or two might be in the mix. But since when do peaceful Cherokees make common cause with Kiowas and Comanches?"

"Ahh, don't peddle that sweet-lavender 'peaceful Cherokee' sheep dip to *this* hoss. In the Cheraw nation, a young buck ain't got no status a-tall 'lessen he kills an enemy or takes a prisoner in battle. The boys are taught how they're dishonored forever if they don't avenge an insult. Hell, a Cheraw buck can't even look at a woman, happens he ain't took a scalp yet. *You'd* be spoiling for war, too, happens it was the only way to get you a little slap 'n' tickle."

Fargo had to concede Jack's main point. Because Cherokees had a written language and formal government, much like the whites, they were called a civilized tribe, not wild Indians. But they had always shown a fiercely warlike nature—to the point, even, of keeping their laws against murder deliberately weak so as not to discourage the killing instinct.

"Their warpath days," Fargo insisted to his trail companion, "were back when they lived east of the Mississippi. Hell, they been peaceful and law-abiding farmers and shepherds since they was forced out here."

"Pipe down, you jay! This child was makin' his beaver while you was still shittin' yellow. The Cheraws have greased for war, count on it."

"It only looks that way," Fargo insisted.

By now Lieutenant Jimmy Briscoe, looking a little sheepish, emerged cautiously from the screening timber behind Fargo. The young officer was so new to the West that he still sunburned easily.

"Sorry, Mr. Fargo," he apologized. "I should've sent out flankers like you advised."

Fargo nodded toward the corpse. "Hell, I'm still sassy, soldier blue. Apologize to him and his kin."

The shavetail flushed to his earlobes. "My orders are clear. Proceed immediately to Sweetwater Creek and rendezvous with Colonel Oglethorpe's group. I was ordered to avoid dividing my force."

The force in question was emerging from cover, their .56 caliber carbines at the ready. It was a small expedition: thirty sharpshooters, two scouts, two Osage Indian interpreters, two mule-drawn supply wagons. One wagon was filled with rations, water, ammunition, and medical supplies. The second hauled forage for the animals.

"Sending out flankers," Fargo advised the green officer, "ain't the same as dividing your force. I recommend it anytime the terrain closes in on you."

For a few moments Fargo was distracted as he watched Yellowstone Jack prepare to mount. The crusty old flint refused to ride a good-natured horse, on the reasoning that politeness was a sign of weakness. So Fargo bit back a grin as Jack stepped into a stirrup. His feisty ginger crow-hopped just as Jack stuck his foot into leather. The old explorer went flat on his sitter, cussing like a stable sergeant.

"Skye," Jack muttered moments later, pointing with his chin toward a break in the trees. Puffs of dark signal smoke drifted against the deep blue morning sky.

"They're warning other braves that we're coming," Fargo said as he grabbed a fistful of the Ovaro mane and swung up into the saddle. "It's still twenty miles to Sweetwater Creek, and some good ambush country. Things're gonna get lively, count on it."

Fargo rode out ahead, sending Yellowstone Jack back to guard their backtrail. Small but frequent canyons and ravines, as well as steep hills, made the terrain difficult for horse and rider. Expanses of deep, loose sand had to be avoided or the wagons would bog down.

Fargo marked a trail for the rest, ever alert to his surroundings, not forgetting that signal smoke earlier. But he also gave some thought to Colonel Lansford Oglethorpe, hero of the Mexican War and outspoken admirer of American Indians. Oglethorpe was convinced that recent grievances, among the many tribes in the Indian Territory, could be settled without warfare.

Thus, riding under a white truce flag, he and several military aides had gone on ahead to meet with tribal representatives at Sweetwater Creek. Fargo was all for the peace road, but considered the plan a fool's play. Colonel Oglethorpe was a popular hero, and if he was killed by Indians, the national wrath would get ugly— and turn against all Indians.

Fargo never stacked his conclusions higher than his evidence. So he still wasn't convinced that a genuine Indian uprising—especially one led by Cherokees— was even taking place in The Nations. But he did know that the reservation system itself was part of the problem because it was so damned illogical.

Most Indians were, by nature, restless people and

confinement only increased that restlessness. Too, not all that long ago this area (the barren buffalo plains beyond the ninety-eighth meridian) was part of vast New Spain, worthless "desert" no one wanted. Now it was arbitrarily declared a homeland for dozens of tribes, many of whom were natural enemies.

The Trailsman's black-and-white stallion picked his way carefully over a hogback, or rocky spine, and now a good view opened up. The terrain out ahead was mostly low hills with scattered pine growth and some steep razorbacks well to the north of the river. In places near the Arkansas, the grass grew high as the knuckles of a full-grown buffalo. Fargo studied all of it a long time, looking for danger.

"Let's head back, old campaigner," he finally said to the Ovaro. "I draw my pay next week, and this nursemaid job is over."

Just as Fargo started to tighten the reins, he heard a distant, mournful howl that made his scalp tighten and tingle. He knew, being a lifelong drifter and trailsman, that it was only the sound of wind whistling through the nearby trees.

But memory brought back the old legends about the Hell Hounds—spectral hounds said to hunt in the wildest part of the woods. If one heard the baying of these hounds, the old legend said, it spelled death to the hearer within a year.

"Sounds mighty close to Sweetwater Creek," Fargo muttered as he reined the Ovaro around, thinking of Colonel Oglethorpe.

Fargo rejoined the main column, which had delayed only long enough to bury poison-dart victim Private Robinson in a humble grave beside the trail.

"Clear trail ahead?" Lieutenant Jimmy Briscoe asked, his voice tense.

Fargo grunted affirmation.

"But the country's not so open around Sweetwater Creek," Fargo added. "In fact, it's perfect ambush country."

"Colonel Oglethorpe rode in under a truce flag," Briscoe said. "And he's a friend to the Indian."

"*The* Indian don't exist," Fargo assured him. "Just many Indians, all with different ideas. Ain't that right, Ten Bears?"

This last question was directed to one of the two Osage interpreters riding beside Jimmy. Between them, Ten Bears and Standing Feather spoke ten Indian languages as well as good English. Yet they could go for days without speaking unless spoken to.

"Red men hate each other more than hate whites," Ten Bears said, ignoring the question. Like his companion, he wore buckskin leg bands trimmed with dyed porcupine quills. "Make war on each other always instead of on whites. This is why we have lost our hunting grounds."

"Hell," Fargo said good-naturedly. "I see you speak good English. When you gonna learn to *listen* to it?"

Whooping hoarsely, Yellowstone Jack came galloping up from the rear of the formation.

"Eyes right!" he shouted to the rest. "Eyes right! God-in-whirlwinds! You'll call me a liar, Skye, happens I just *tell* you!"

The Arkansas, spilling over its low banks, formed a wide, shallow waterway just below them, a complex series of interconnecting pools and backwaters.

Fargo spotted a lone Cherokee expertly paddling a light, flat-bottomed bateau across a wide pool. The craft's tapered ends and shallow draw let it skim and mudbanks and allowed steady progress with easy paddling.

"I don't credit my own eyes!" Jack added. He began swearing with evident pleasure, a string of foul and creative eipithets that made even the Ovaro blush. "It's more of that goddamn petticoat gov'ment, is what it is. This is what comes from them damn Cheraws allowing women at war councils."

The Cherokee paddling the bateau was a female, and a true beauty at that.

"She's a Ghighau," Fargo told a staring Jimmy. "Means 'Beloved Women.' You'll also hear 'em called War Women. Besides fighting in battles, their job is to prepare the secret Black Drink that's taken before battle."

"Fighting in battle? A woman that easy to look at?" the young officer remarked. "Man! She's beautiful, and almost . . . regal. Somebody should paint her."

Fargo had to agree as he continued to watch the War Woman. She spotted the men up above and back-paddled a stroke to halt the bateau's easy glide, glancing up toward the trail.

The young woman's long jet hair was combed close to her head and held in back with a silver clasp. Fargo took in the huge, almond-shaped eyes, the fine Roman nose, the full lips that made him think of berries heavy with juice. His eyes cut to the tanned, exposed skin between her short jacket and skirt—it looked taut as a drumhead.

"*Paint* her?" Yellowstone Jack repeated, scorn coloring his tone. "*Plant* her, you mean. Look closer into that bateau, Lieutenant."

Fargo had already spotted what Jack meant: one of the huge Cherokee bows that could hurl an arrow four hundred yards, and one of the deadly rifled blowguns used to fire poison darts like the one that killed Pvt. Robinson.

"Beautiful Death Bringer," Fargo remarked.

"The hell you babbling?" Jack demanded.

"That's what her Cherokee name means in English," Fargo explained, "if that's the same woman I've heard spoken of at Fort Covage and Fort Smith. Her English name is Sarah something or other. And she's an official Indian princess by right of birth."

Yellowstone Jack snorted. "Save your breath to cool your porridge," he scoffed. "I know 'B' from a bull's foot, and them ain't 'royal trappings' your princess is hauling. Matter fact, that very blowgun coulda done for Robinson. Ah, t'hell with this chinwag."

Jack reached for the .38 caliber magazine pistol in his sash.

"Not a good idea," Fargo warned. "A War Woman is best left alone."

"Ahh, purty little thing, she won't want to muss her hair. I'll just put a hole in her boat, under the waterline," Jack said. "Force her to nose in."

However, he never got his shot off. Moving with catlike speed, she pulled a quartz-tipped arrow from a quiver of soft fox skin. With deft fingers she notched it on her sinew-string bow and sent the arrow fwipping.

"Great jumpin' Judas!" Yellowstone Jack roared out as his beaver hat seemed to leap off his head.

Fargo, sporting an admiring grin, watched the arrow thwack into a nearby tree. It quivered for a few seconds with the force of its suddenly interrupted energy.

"That's one petticoat you best leave alone, hoss," Fargo advised him. "And don't snatch up that rifle, *you* started the trouble by dropping a bead on her. This is her home, not ours."

Fargo turned toward Jimmy Briscoe, who, like his men, was still staring in amazement at the receding Cherokee princess.

"Sweetwater Creek is about ten miles farther," Fargo said. "I got a hunch somebody hopes to make it there before we do. Since the trail is wide, I recommend advancing in columns of four to discourage ambush."

"Yessir," the kid said obediently, for Skye Fargo was the most celebrated contract scout the army ever hired.

Fargo seldom got bossy with young officers, not wanting to weaken their authority with the men. But lives were possibly on the line now, and this well-intended kid was brand-well to a command position.

"Place every man under orders of strict silence as we advance the last few miles," Fargo added. "Remove your saber, Jimmy, so it doesn't rattle. Any man who needs to cough or sneeze must cover his head in a blanket first."

Jimmy left to convey these orders. Yellowstone Jack turned toward the tree behind him to remove the arrow and his hat.

"Shit, piss, and corruption!" the crotchety old explorer exclaimed, staring at the gnarled bark of the tree. "Fargo, come glom this and *then* tell me the Cheraws ain't struck the war trail."

Fargo did look. Just below the embedded arrow, three fresh notches had been carved into the tree—a message from some Indian courier. But it had been a long time since Fargo had seen this distinctive pattern: three parallel lines slanting from right to left.

His face suddenly felt cold. "Jesus," he almost whispered, recalling that death omen from earlier. "Looks like the Cherokee Keetoowah is back."

"A-huh. The secret Nighthawk Society," Jack affirmed. "The bloodiest bunch of killers ever got up by any band of red devils. A Nighthawk knows fifty ways to kill a man before breakfast. And we might soon be riding right into their midst. Happens a man wants to get his life over quick, he only needs to throw in with Skye Fargo."

No other series has this much historical action!

THE TRAILSMAN

**Available wherever books are sold or at
penguin.com**